Con mucho cariño
para Jacinta, que
siempre seas un orgullo
para tus padres y
que nunca olvides
lo fantástica
que eres.

Los mejores deseos,

Sandra López-Rocha

Feb 12 2015

Para el alumno o la alumna que lo merezca:

HOW TO DEFEND YOURSELF AGAINST SCORPIONS

FERNANDO SORRENTINO,

con mis saludos.

Bristol, marzo 2014

red rattle
BOOKS

How To Defend Yourself Against Scorpions

2013

Copyright of this collection of short stories
© Fernando Sorrentino

All stories are printed with the permission of the author

Translations are acknowledged on a separate page.

Red Rattle Books thanks the translators for allowing
Red Rattle Books to use their translations.

A CIP catalogue number for this book is
available from the British Library

ISBN 978-1-909086-04-3

Printed and bound by Anchor Print

Front and back cover and
artwork by Robin Castle

Published by Red Rattle Books

LIST OF CONTENTS

TRANSLATIONS

Mere Suggestion Translation by Clark M. Zlotchew

Method For Defence Against Scorpions
Translation by Clark M. Zlotchew

A Life Perhaps Worth Restoring Translation by Emmy Briggs

A Lifestyle Translation by Gustavo Artiles

A Question Of Age Translation by Michele McKay Aynesworth

An Enlightening Book
Translation by Gustavo Artiles and Alex Patterson

Chastisement By The Lambs
Translation by Gustavo Artiles and Alex Patterson

Doctor Moreau Did It Translation by Michele McKay Aynesworth

Engineer Sismondi's Notebook Translation by Gustavo Artiles

Piccirilli Translation by Gustavo Artiles

Episode of Don Francisco Figueredo Translation by Gustavo Artiles

Essence And Attribute Translation by Clark M. Zlotchew

Habits Of The Artichoke Translation by Michele McKay Aynesworth

Illegitimate Ambitions Translated by Gustavo Artiles

Problem Solved Translation by Jonathan Cole

Rewarding Superstitions Translation by Clark M. Zlotchew

The Cubelli Lagoon Translation by Michele McKay Aynesworth

The Empire of The Cotorritas
Translation by Gustavo Artiles and Alex Patterson

The Library Of Mabel Translation by Gustavo Artiles

There's A Man In The Habit Of Hitting Me On The Head With An Umbrella
Translation by Clark M. Zlotchew

The Ushuala Rabbit Translation by Michele McKay Aynesworth

The Visitation
Translation by Norman Thomas di Giovanni and Susan Ashe

Two Common Misconceptions Translation by Donald A Yates

Unjustified Fears Translation by Naomi Lindstrom

Waiting For A Resolution Translation by Susan Ashe

HOW TO DEFEND YOURSELF AGAINST SCORPIONS

FERNANDO SORRENTINO

FOREWORD

For about forty years, Fernando Sorrentino has been nourishing Argentine literature with rare, uncanny, witty and funny stories. Born in 1942 in Buenos Aires where he still lives and writes, Fernando has created a strange kind of fiction within our letters. The result is an impressive corpus of almost 60 books, most of them collections of short stories, although a novel, a novela, a range of stories for children and the classic 'Seven Conversations With Jorge Luis Borges' are also part of his output.

It is in the field of the short story, though, that Sorrentino has proved to be fecund and successful. Personal invasions in any of its different expressions, revenge and the gradual accumulation of daily absurd sequences occur often in the stories included in the key collections: *Imperios y servidumbres* (1972), *El mejor de los mundos posibles* (1976), *El rigor de las desdichas* (1994), *Existe un hombre que tiene la costumbre de pegarme con un paraguas en la cabeza* (2005), *El regreso* (2005) and *El crimen de san Alberto* (2008). In the most recent of them, we find the narrator at his best. Mystery, humour, realism, allegories and fantasy coexist in the stories, some of them true masterpieces like 'The Visitation,' 'There's A Man In The Habit Of Hitting Me On The Head With An Umbrella,' 'Mere Suggestion' and 'Problem Solved'.

Fortunately, those stories are also included in this generous selection, together with other masterworks such as 'Waiting For A Resolution,' 'Two Common Misconceptions,' 'Unjustified Fears,' 'A Lifestyle' and 'An Enlightening Book.' Many of them have been translated to different languages, including Finnish, Hungarian, Polish, Bulgarian, Chinese, Persian, Japanese, Turkish, Vietnamese, Tamil and Kabyle.

In these tales, we frequently encounter events typical of the Laurel and Hardy films in which, little by little, plain circumstances grow into situations of colossal proportions.

The tone, however, resembles that of the old silent movies of Buster Keaton where, unperturbed, the actor faces the adversities of real life in its irreversible absurdity.

Although critics find deep meanings in the work of Sorrentino, there is no moral or philosophical intention in his writing. He cheerfully writes for the sake of writing. This results in marvellous and odd situations that reveal what the narrator discovers after placing his skeptical magnifier on apparently simple human situations, the weirdness of this funny world.

Fernando Sorrentino is not only a literature professor but has a great knowledge of the Spanish language and a love for words. His writing is precise and rigorous. The adjectives are accurate, and the syntax of his agile prose logical and musical. Reviewers have stated that his works clearly fit into the Argentinean tradition of short stories mastered by Jorge Luis Borges, Julio Cortázar and Marco Denevi. In numerous interviews and essays, our writer identifies these authors as reference points.

Other influences can be traced to Spanish literature and the picaresque novels of Miguel de Cervantes Saavedra and Francisco de Quevedo where the hunger of the anti-hero is essential to the story. The Spanish word *pícaro* means 'rogue.' Charles Dickens and the 'idolatrized' Franz Kafka have also influenced the imagination and writing of Sorrentino.

The stories included in this anthology were lucky to find translators who do justice to his art. There is no room in this book for the traitorous translator, the *traduttore, traditore* axiom.

Stories by Fernando Sorrentino have been copiously translated into the English language. 'How To Defend

Yourself Against Scorpions,' though, is the first full volume to offer a comprehensive spectrum of the author's talent, his particular and peculiar world. An audience whose literary tradition includes names such as Saki, Jerome K. Jerome, P. G. Wodehouse and Max Beerbohm will surely enjoy and praise the voice of this gifted South American writer.

Juan José Delaney
Universidad del Salvador
Buenos Aires, Argentina

MERE SUGGESTION

My friends say I am very suggestible. I think they're right. As evidence of this, they bring up a little incident that I was involved in last Thursday.

That morning, I was reading a horror novel and, although it was broad daylight, I fell victim to the power of suggestion. This suggestion implanted in me the idea that there was a bloodthirsty murderer in the kitchen and this bloodthirsty murderer, brandishing an enormous dagger, was waiting for me to enter the kitchen so he could leap upon me and plunge the knife into my back. So, in spite of my being seated directly across from the kitchen door, in spite of the fact that no one could have gone into the kitchen without my having seen him and that there was no other access to the kitchen but that door. In spite of all these facts, I, nonetheless, was fully convinced that the murderer lurked behind the closed door.

So I fell victim to the power of suggestion and did not have the courage to enter the kitchen. This worried me because lunchtime was approaching and it would be indispensable for me to go into the kitchen. Then the doorbell rang.

'Come in!' I yelled without standing up. 'It's not locked.'

The building superintendent came in with two or three letters.

'My leg fell asleep,' I said. 'Could you go to the kitchen and bring me a glass of water?'

The super said, 'Of course,' opened the kitchen door and went in. I heard a cry of pain and the sound of a body that, in collapsing, dragged with it dishes or bottles. Then I leaped from my chair and ran to the kitchen. The super, half his body on the table and an enormous dagger plunged into his back, lay dead. Now, calmed down, I was able to determine that, of course, there was no murderer in the kitchen.

As is logical, it was a case of mere suggestion.

METHOD FOR DEFENCE AGAINST SCORPIONS

People are surprised, fearful and even indignant over the considerable proliferation of scorpions which threatens Buenos Aires, a city which until quite recently had been entirely free of this particular genus of arachnid.

Unimaginative individuals have recourse to an overly traditional method of defence against the scorpions, the employment of poisons. The more imaginative fill their houses with toads, frogs and lizards in the hope that they will devour the scorpions. Both groups fail abominably. The scorpions firmly refuse to ingest poisons, while the reptiles refuse to ingest scorpions. Both groups, in their ineptness and haste, succeed in one thing only, to exacerbate even more, if possible, the hatred which scorpions profess toward all humanity.

I have a different method. I have attempted unsuccessfully to disseminate it, like all trailblazers I am misunderstood. I believe my method to be, in all modesty, not only the best but the only possible method of defence against the scorpions.

Its basic principle consists of avoiding a direct confrontation, of engaging in brief but risky skirmishes, of concealing our enmity from the scorpions. (Of course, I know that one must proceed with caution, I know that the sting of a scorpion is fatal. It is true that if I were to stuff myself into a diving suit, I would be completely safe from the scorpion. It is no less true that if I were to do that, the scorpions would know with complete certainty that I fear them. And I am very much afraid of scorpions. But one mustn't lose his equanimity.)

An elementary measure, one, which is effective while free from overemphasis on violence and ominous theatricals, is composed of two simple steps. The first is to tie the cuffs of my trousers with very taut rubber bands, this is to prevent the scorpions from crawling up my legs. The second is to pretend that I suffer greatly from cold and to wear a pair of leather gloves at all times, this is to avoid being stung on the hands. (More than one negative spirit has pointed out only the disadvantages that this method entails in the summer without recognizing its undeniable and more general merits.) The head, however, should be left uncovered; this is the best way of presenting the scorpions with a brave and optimistic image of ourselves. Besides, scorpions are not normally in the habit of hurling themselves from the ceiling onto the human face although at times they do. (This, at any rate, is what happened to my late neighbour, the mother of four cunning little kiddies, now orphans. To make matters worse, these facts give rise to erroneous theories, which only serve to make the struggle against the scorpions more arduous and troublesome. As a matter of fact, the surviving husband, with no adequate scientific basis, affirms that the six scorpions were attracted by the intensely blue colour of the victim's eyes and adduces as flimsy proof of such a rash assertion the fact, totally fortuitous, that the stings were distributed in groups of three to each pupil. I honestly believe that this is a mere superstition dreamed up by the cowardly mind of this pusillanimous individual.)

When on the defence it is necessary to pretend to be unaware of the existence of the scorpions while attacking them. As though by accident, I, as cool as could be, managed to kill from eighty to a hundred scorpions every day. I proceed in the following manner, which, for the survival of the human race, I hope will be imitated and, if possible, perfected.

Appearing distracted, I sit down in the kitchen and begin to read the newspaper. Every once in a while, I look at my watch and mumble to myself in a voice loud enough to be heard by the scorpions, 'Damn! Why the devil doesn't Pérez call?' Pérez' undependability angers me and provides the excuse to stamp my feet wrathfully on the floor a few times. In this way, I massacre no less than ten of the innumerable scorpions which cover the floor. At irregular intervals, I repeat my expression of impatience and in this manner I manage to kill quite a large number. This is not to say that I slight the equally innumerable scorpions, which completely cover the ceiling and the walls (which are five quivering throbbing shifting black seas). From time to time, I feign an attack of hysteria and hurl some heavy object against the wall, not neglecting to keep cursing that damned Pérez for taking so long to call. It's a shame that I've already broken several sets of cups and dishes and that I live among dented pots and pans but the price of defending oneself from the scorpions is high. At last, someone inevitably calls. 'It's Pérez!' I shout and rush to the phone. Naturally, my haste and my anxiousness are such that I fail to notice the thousands upon thousands of scorpions, which softly carpet the floor and burst underfoot with the gelatinously harsh sound of an egg being cracked. At times but only at times, it wouldn't do to overindulge in this recourse, I trip and fall full length thus appreciably enlarging the area of my impact and, consequently, the number of dead scorpions. When I get to my feet once more my clothes are completely decorated with the sticky corpses of a great many scorpions, detaching them one by one is a delicate task but one, which allows me to savour my triumph.

Now, I'd like to indulge in a short digression in order to relate an anecdote, enlightening in itself, concerning an incident that happened to me some days ago and in which, without intending to do so, I played a heroic role, if I say so myself.

It was lunchtime. As usual, I found the table covered with scorpions, the silverware covered with scorpions, the stove covered with scorpions. With patience, with resignation, with my eyes averted, I gradually pushed them off and on to the floor. Since the struggle against the scorpions consumes the greater part of my time, I decided to fix myself a fast meal, a few fried eggs. There I was, eating them, every so often pushing aside some particularly bold scorpion that had climbed up on the table or that was walking on my knees when, from the ceiling, an especially vigorous and robust scorpion fell or jumped on to my plate.

Petrified, I dropped my knife and fork. How was I to interpret that behaviour? Was it merely a chance occurrence? an attack on my person?, a test? I remained perplexed for some instants. What were the scorpions' intentions toward me? Being a seasoned soldier in the battle against them, I understood immediately. They wanted to force me to modify my method of defence, to make me decidedly shift to the offensive. But I was very sure of the effectiveness of my strategy; they would not succeed in tricking me.

With repressed rage, I saw the scorpion's thick hairy legs splashing in the eggs, I saw its body becoming impregnated with yellow, I saw the venomous tail waving in the air like a shipwrecked sailor calling for help. Objectively considered, the scorpion's death struggle constituted a beautiful spectacle. But it made me a bit nauseous. I almost bungled it. I thought of tossing the contents of the plate into the incinerator. Still, I have a great deal of will power and managed to restrain myself in time. If I had not, I would have earned the abhorrence and the reproof of the thousands upon thousands of scorpions, which, with renewed suspicion, were watching me from the ceiling, the walls, the floor, the stove and the lamps. Then, they would have had a pretext to consider themselves under attack, and who knows what could have occurred.

I steeled myself and, pretending not to notice the scorpion that was still struggling in my plate, I ate it distractedly together with the egg and even mopped the plate with a crust of bread in order not to leave even one bit of scorpion and egg. It turned out to be not as repugnant as I had feared. Just a trifle acid perhaps but that sensation might have been due to the fact that my palate was still unaccustomed to the ingestion of scorpions. With the last mouthful, I smiled with satisfaction. Later, it occurred to me that the scorpion's shell, tougher than I would have liked, might cause me indigestion, so delicately, in order not to offend the rest of the scorpions, I drank a glass of Alka Seltzer.

There are other variants of this method but, and this is the crux of it, it is necessary to remember that it is essential to proceed as if one were unaware of the presence, better yet, the existence, of the scorpions. Even so, I am now assaulted by some doubts. I think the scorpions have begun to realize that my attacks are not accidents. Yesterday, when I dropped a pot of boiling water on the floor, I noticed that from the refrigerator door some three or four hundred scorpions were observing me rancorously, suspiciously, reprovingly.

Maybe my method, too, is destined to fail. But, for now, I cannot think of any better method of defending myself from the scorpions.

A LIFE PERHAPS
WORTH RESTORING

1. I am the subject of an assault

Like everyone else, I have my own phobias and manias. I am obsessed by cleanliness. I like animals but only in the zoo or in museums. I do not touch, nor do I allow myself to be touched, by dogs or cats. I do everything I can to eliminate spiders or insects at home. I cannot even stand the zooming by of a fly or a mosquito. Fine.

A rotten potato was an alarming sign, the certain presence of no less than a mouse or, even worse, a rat, in my small apartment. But, where? Where?

How could it have gotten in? A stupid question, which deserved an intelligent question as a reply, how could it not have gotten in?

A rotten potato, that was all. But the pest was somewhere in the apartment, and this certainty forced me to start an extremely disagreeable series of actions to find the mouse, following an initial optimistic impulse to believe that it was a mouse and not a rat and, by whatever means possible with minimal direct intervention on my part, kill it and then, without touching it by means of broom and dust pan, throw it in the trash, take the trash bag to the sidewalk and let the trash collector truck take it far from my home, take it where they compress and bury all waste and debris.

Trembling with anticipated revolt, I went searching with a broomstick through every nook and cranny. I picked up curtain hems, rescued shoes that, no longer used, lay forgotten in their graves. Volume by volume, I dismantled my whole library and renewed acquaintances with so many books that had once interested me and which I would never read again. I dusted off old clothes, which now looked ridiculous to me.

And so did I pass that first sterile day like a diligent and suspicious ferret. I believe I conducted a diligent and exhaustive inspection of my whole apartment which, let it be said, is quite small. It only consists of kitchen, bathroom, dining and bedroom, none of which is too spacious.

A bachelor, I live alone, have lunch and dinner in my kitchen and try to create the least possible disruption. This is why, for the most part, I resort to simple meals bought at delis, such as breaded cutlets or meat pies. On other even more austere occasions, I get by with bread and cold cuts. As you can see, I do not like, nor do I want, to cook. It is just a way of wasting time and effort.

I rarely use more than one plate, one glass, one fork and one knife. As soon as I am done eating, I wash these four items using boiling water and detergent and I leave them bottom up in the sink. I could even say that for years I have been using these same four items.

Nonetheless, just for fun and because I love them, I like to fry a fresh batch of potatoes from time to time. This is why I usually have some potatoes stored in a spotlessly clean green plastic drawer. Never more than a kilo. I want to clarify that these few potatoes are the only edible product, aside from those in airtight containers, which can be found in my home. Logically, what I found was a rotten potato.

We all know that a refrigerator is foolproof. No mouse could ever open its door to pilfer the few items I store inside: a couple of steaks, a bag of hotdogs, a small anchovy jar, another one with green olives, a piece of fresh cheese, two or three tomatoes, a stick of butter, some fruit and nothing else.

I prefer to buy strictly the bare essentials and thus avoid accumulating foodstuff as it may go rancid before I can eat it. True, this habit forces me to multiply my shopping trips but in compensation it gives me two advantages: not to be forced to eat what I do not wish to just because it is there, and it forces me, pleasantly, to go out on the Villa Urquiza Streets on a daily basis. This is something I like and I need since I spend long hours locked up at home dedicated to my work.

2. A certain independence

For a long time now, and I hope for the rest of my life, I have been working as a translator. To get there, I had to go through three difficult changes in my career: that of an office worker, that of a Spanish and literature teacher and that of an advertising editor. I won't even try to describe such jobs. I will say, though, that I felt uncomfortable in all of them; culturally, economically and ethically, in the strict order I have named them.

My activities were diverse but my personality and tastes were always the same.

What I enjoyed doing was reading. And I read throughout most of my free time. I even read while riding buses and the underground. Thus, I believe I must have read for years and years at an average of one hundred pages a day. Since I have a good memory and an excellent capacity for idea association, my reading was enriched by relating, resonances and deep thinking. I thus learned a lot of things, the majority of which had absolutely no practical application. It doesn't matter. I have always felt sorry for those people who are *only* practical.

Among the things I learned was to be able to read in various languages. *To read,* not to speak, which is something altogether different.

For sheer pleasure and amusement, I translated stories by Wells, Wilde, Melville, Hudson; I translated hundreds of pages from nineteenth century English writers, Dickens, Thackeray, Meredith.

And then, or maybe simultaneously, I jumped over to French. I translated Camus, Claudel, Flaubert, Maupassant and who knows how many others.

I realized that, knowing two languages, it was quite easy to learn a third one and a fourth one and a fifth one.

The wonderfully difficult thing to achieve was to make the Spanish version not to read as a translation. Unwittingly at first and by bits and pieces, I automatically began to paraphrase syntactic constructions from the English language into Spanish. I realized that the apparent similarity with Italian was deceitful and that quite often there were problems requiring lots of reworking and imagination. I had, and still have, lots of problems with German whereas I had little trouble with French. Simplifying, I would daresay that French can be translated into Spanish *almost* word for word.

As a natural result of these toils, there came a day I started translating books for several publishing houses.

After some sort of assessment, I saw the opportunity to gain a priceless advantage, that of my almost total freedom. The price of becoming my own lord and master. No more administrative bosses, inept deans, nor smiling executives. I didn't think twice. I resigned from the last eight hours of professorship I had left and started translating full time.

For the first time in my life, I felt relatively happy working. I was thirty-four years old and had been fearful of not having found a niche for myself in this world. That was eleven years ago.

I cannot deny I am satisfied with myself. As I have said, I have acquired a sort of skill or habit in the different languages I deal with. Since I type accurately and rather fast, I usually cover a lot of ground in a short time. This allows me to earn relatively well and get paid quite frequently.

My dining room has become my desk, the place where I work, where I like to be. All walls are covered with books from floor to ceiling except the wall with window doors leading to the balcony. As the years go by, I become closer to some of my books and grow apart from others, which does not mean I have re-read them. Sometimes I just read for pleasure but most of the time I work on translations.

I have a fruitful routine, in general terms. I place the original book to my left, I place a sheet of carbon paper between two sheets of writing paper in the typewriter and an ashtray to my right. I work from eight to twelve. I drink 'mate' and I cannot quit the damned smoking habit, something I swear to do on a nightly basis.

I then have a light lunch and take a nap for about an hour. I go back to translating from three to seven p.m. At this time, I go shopping or out for a walk, read stuff I like, go to a movie or meet Elsa with whom I have an irregular longtime relationship, which has no future. I know she wants to marry me. I don't see the need to and would prefer not to alter my way of life.

Above all, I translate from books in English. They are usually North American and cover subjects that do not interest me or which I flat out reject, pedagogy, sociology and psychoanalysis. Quite often, they begin with a page of acknowledgments, the author thanks Professor So and So who formulated interesting observations, Doctor So and So who suggested this wonderful thing; to Miss So and So who was kind enough to type the whole manuscript. This kind of rubbish annoys me but I translate it righteously even though I ask myself what is the use of it all. I am sure the reader will carelessly skip over them.

And yet, I realize now what has led me to minutely recount these details of my daily grey routine. I did not want to talk about this but rather about the story that begins with the episode of the rotten potato. But one thing leads to another albeit not deliberately. Doubtless, I was trying to show I am an extremely methodical person and, why not, an efficient one.

At home, everything is neat and polished to a fanatical degree. I take a shower and shave every day, I shower twice in summertime, my clothes are always impeccably clean and pressed at the laundry. I cannot press except for square or rectangular pieces like napkins and handkerchiefs. I even find time to put shoe polish on my shoes every night and to buff them every morning.

As I have said, except for the above mentioned kilo of potatoes, you will not find any kind of edible stuff in my home.

So, the question is, why me? A maniac for cleanliness and order, why should I have to suffer the intrusion of a rat in my apartment?

From here onwards, it will no longer be a mouse, it will be a rat.

3. Defensive Strategies

No one will answer this question. It is useless to complain about destiny's plans. But there was something quite clear, I had to find and kill the damned rat as soon as possible.

There is a saying that goes, 'less clutter, less stress.' I started throwing things I no longer used in a plastic bag, four pairs of old shoes. This small move set up an explosive punishing expedition against all the things I was no longer using and which were there just as mere heirlooms representing laziness and apathy—old pullovers, a ridiculous summer cap, worn scarves, old fashioned ties. Thusly, I filled six plastic trash bags.

I never found out the last name of my cleaning lady, her first name singles her out on its own. 'Nicanora.' And to Nicanora, who lives far away from me, and I suppose in indigence, I gave away all these clothes. She gladly accepted them and took them away in three trips, two bags at a time. She thus liberated me of those useless things. My closet suddenly became quite spacious.

Meanwhile, I threw the rest of the potatoes in the trashcan, I washed the green plastic drawer with hot water and bleach and put it to dry in the hot evening sun on my balcony. In the evening, I bought another kilo of potatoes, rinsed the dirt out of them with water, dried them with a dishtowel and stored them in the fridge.

At this point, I could rightfully assert there were no other edible substances inside the whole apartment. This cleaning operation constituted my first attack against the rat, a means to ask it to retreat in pursuit of more nourishing regions.

4. Attack plan and first skirmish

There is a veterinary clinic called 'My Puppy' a block and a half away from home. Sometimes, I stop to look through the window; they sell puppies, kitties, fish and turtles. Exhibited but not for sale are a small lizard, a spider and a snake.

Not satisfied with my prior precautionary measures, I went into the place and asked for professional advice on the safest and most efficient method to get rid of rats.

A woman wearing a green apron was sitting behind a desk and using a calculator. Only after I finished talking and a silent pause did she condescend to get up and come to the counter. This kind of indifference irked me and predisposed me against her.

She had, nonetheless, heard and understood my question quite well. She spoke with a nasal voice, unpleasantly articulated, showing small serrated teeth underneath or on top of her enormous gums. Her lips contorted in a vicious smile during the most lethal part of her discourse.

She recommended some rat pills that looked appetizing, that is to the rats, and which they would avidly swallow without ever suspecting that the core of such delicacy hid a poisonous trap that would send them to the next world.

I felt an irresistible impulse to interject some kind of objection; this woman was disagreeable.

'Fine,' I said. 'But let's suppose the rat dies in an unreachable hole. Sooner or later, a decomposition process will start, and how will I be able to stand that awful smell and the idea of coexisting with the rotting carcass of a rat?'

'My dear Sir,' she replied smugly, 'you seem to live in the Stone Age. How old are you, if I may ask?'

'Forty-five,' I managed to respond.

'You were already in fourth grade when I was still suckling,' she replied. 'That's why you are not aware of the latest scientific advances.'

Since I did not reply, she continued:

'These pills,' she held the box between index and thumb, 'do not work as you erroneously believe. To start with, they have no venom and, by themselves, they cannot kill anyone. They act indirectly. They produce a decalcifying effect, thus, when the rat falls or hits something, it will suffer a fracture in one or more bones. It will become paralyzed, unable to search for food. Thus, little by little, it will end up dying of starvation.'

She fixed me with an almost ferocious stare; I could barely hold it.

'Now, there is the second and false problem stated by you, the animal's decomposition with the subsequent stench, worms etc., after effects. None of this will happen. These pills have a taxidermic drug, which will impede rotting of the carcass, so much so, that any given day you will have the pleasure of owning an embalmed rat. A pet you can place on your night table.'

Although I would have preferred a less grotesque and scientific, less Anglo-Saxon, plan, something a bit more trustful like facing the rat and trying to kill it by hitting it on the head with a shovel, for instance, I accepted her satanic prescription because, truly, I no longer had the strength or the will to start a face to face confrontation.

I went back home and dedicated myself to strategically distributing the repulsive brown pills close to the baseboards. In spite of their clean ascetic look, I was shivering and revolted.

In short, I had spent most of the day trying to implement measures against the rat. This had altered my usual living scheme, and it bothered me no end.

By nightfall, I thought it was time to get my life back on track. I had already done everything possible to get rid of the intruder, and it felt right to return to my everyday activities. Therefore, I went to bed with a clear conscience and two books, the original *Crime And Punishment* in Russian, and the Spanish version rendered by Rafael Cansinos Assens in 1935. As a pastime, before going to sleep, I compared the original vs. the translation, phrase by phrase, of an episode, which had always seduced me. I refer to the sixth section of Chapter II wherein Judge Porfirii gets confused and accuses Raskolnikow.

This was a pleasant task, and it seemed to pull me out of my surrounding reality. And yet in a blurry and latent way I could not stop thinking that somewhere in the house the damned rat was perhaps very close to me. The pleasant side prevailed in my conscience nonetheless and lazily, slowly, I fell asleep. I still had time to turn off the light on my night table.

At some point during the night, I woke up. I remained still, expectant. I heard some rhythmic noises, like someone trying to tap a pen against a wooden surface.

'It's the rat!' I whispered nervously while turning on the light on my night table at the same time.

My room showed up, and the taps stopped. Still and attentive, I thought of the rat, motionless, its ears perked up, trying to figure out where danger or death, announced by the sudden light, was coming from.

It was 2:07 a.m. I turned off the light on my night table at 2:12, feeling sure that the taps would come back immediately. I had a plan. Guided by the taps, I would move in the dark through my familiar home until I located the whereabouts of the rat. I would then suddenly turn on the lights and kill her with a single stroke, armed with whatever was at hand.

After a long time in the dark, I had to admit that the rat had opted to remain cautiously still. It was then that my cautiously planned strategy changed into that of an irrational fighter. In some kind of a frenzied attack, I jumped out of bed, turned on all the lights in the house, grabbed a broom and roughly ransacked the whole apartment, slamming and banging included.

I found nothing, absolutely nothing.

Nervous and perspiring, looking ridiculous in my boxers and slippers, I sat in the kitchen to grab a smoke and to think. There was nothing much to reflect on, though. A rat is a small animal, agile and slick, cunning and malleable, an animal that runs, jumps, climbs, hides and is superbly prepared to fight for its life. It could hide in a thousand unthinkable invisible corners and I, a huge, clumsy, noisy and massive pachyderm, would not be able to find it.

With the last puff from my cigarette, I resolved to consider the rat episode as concluded. I went to bed and I slept. I never knew if the tapping noise came back.

The alarm clock went off at 7:00 am. Half asleep, I already had a well-defined purpose. Under no circumstance would I allow the intruder to interfere or distort my usual activities, my normal life. I had to adhere to my usual activities and wait. Just wait with no further activity on my part. Sooner or later, I thought, those damned brown pills from the vet would destroy its bones, paralyze it. They would kill it by starvation, embalm it and turn it into a museum rat. I should, therefore, go back to my everyday tasks and not allow the vermin to steal my thoughts or my time, which I could use for more agreeable and useful tasks.

True, right, but how could I remain indifferent before these five small whitish eggs which had just scared me? They were lying there on top of the kitchen table beside the ashtray, which, contrary to my daily cleaning habits, still showed the cigarette butt on top.

Rats are mammals, not oviparous. The drama therefore had acquired another slant, the intruder was not a rat.

Neither could it be a bird. Those are not creatures in the habit of being inside or in corners. By elimination, therefore, it had to be a reptile, a snake, a viper, a lizard?

Unspeakably apprehensive, I rolled a newspaper and used it to push the small reptile eggs until they fell noisily into an empty coffee tin I sometimes use as a pencil holder.

I washed the table top with disinfectant soap and boiled water immediately. I also washed the marble kitchen counter, top and bottom. Also the sink bowl, the walls and the floor. Who knows what kind of repulsive animal had slithered its viscous body over my dear familiar areas? (I knew reptiles are not viscous but rather quite dry and clean but I mentally insisted on this gruesome 'viscous' detail.)

I realized it was past ten in the morning, and I had not even started my everyday work.

At this point, I had two possibilities, a) start working as usual and pretend to ignore the problem, or b) stop working and fully dedicate myself to finding a devastating and definitive solution.

5. Nené's Interference

I know myself well and I do not like prolonging undesirable situations. A few minutes later, I made an appearance at 'My Pet Veterinary,' carrying the five small eggs inside the coffee can.

'What brings you here?' said the woman in a green work coat without raising her eyes from her calculator. 'I see you are in trouble again.'

To me, she was not the type of person I could engage in conversation with, I don't mean a nice conversation just a half way logical one. Therefore, I merely said,

'Could you determine the kind of animal these eggs belong to?'

She violently dumped the contents of the can on her left palm,

'I must tell you I am not a zoologist, I am a veterinarian. However, truth can be accessed through various routes, don't you think?'

She pierced my eyes with hers, like trying to force a response out of me. I hinted a gesture of agreement.

'Some people achieve wisdom,' she went on, 'by means of accumulating information. Others, instead, ponder about things incessantly. I do both things at the same time. I complement my daily studies with serene deliberation. I pretend I am involved with bills and a calculator, while I am really reflecting on man and his destiny.'

She extended both hands, closed.

'Let's see, guess, where are the yararacusú eggs?'

Foolishly, I signalled towards her left hand. She opened it.

'Nothing here,' she smiled contentedly, showing her huge gums and small teeth. 'One to zero, I win. Here are the eggs.'

She opened her right hand and rolled them over the counter.

'What kind of yararacusú eggs are you talking about? Look, these marbles are not an animal's eggs, just that, marbles. Glass marbles, the type kids play around with. When

I was a kid I read Mexican comics and they used to call the marbles 'canicas', remember?'

She was banging them violently with the butt of a paper cutter.

'See? They don't break. They're not eggs, they're marbles.'

I grabbed them, felt them, banged them and I had to admit that the woman was right. I felt suddenly ill as if dizzy or on the verge of fainting.

'I see your pressure has gone down. Have a drink of brandy. Take it, trust me, it will be good for you.' I heard.

All of a sudden, I found myself sitting on a chair in front of a desk on the other side of the counter. The woman had my coat in her hands and she was going through my pockets.

'You're going to have to tell me everything. My name is Maria Inés but everyone calls me Nené. I saw in your ID that your name is Carlos Conforte. Carlos, just like Carlos Gardel. You are also dark-haired and have green eyes that are rare. You have beautiful eyes, Carlitos. Tell me all about it, Carlitos, I can help you. Trust me, Carlitos.'

I felt spiritually diminished and overwhelmed by the woman's ill advised language. The fact was I let myself be carried away by the events and told Nené a very similar story to the one you have just now read in full detail. She became interested in some details of my recent past and asked some precise and intelligent questions about my activities as a clerical worker, as a high school teacher and as an advertising editor.

'Talk to me, Carlitos,' she would say every now and then, stroking my hair. 'I have studied psychoanalysis and I know that talking will do you good.'

I was sitting on a chair, holding the brandy glass in my hand. She was standing by my side and continued to stroke my hair. Suddenly, I reacted, trying to become myself again:

'I am leaving.' I said, getting vertical.

'Hold on a second, it is almost noon. Put on your jacket, it is cold. I'll close the shop, and let's go have lunch together in your apartment. Afterwards, we can have a quick nap in your bed, huh?'

As in a dream, I found myself on Airpurúa Street. Nené and I walked home, went up in the elevator and we had a terrible or beautiful lunch consisting of crackers with butter, salami and red wine mixed with Coca-Cola. We then took a nap up until about five pm.

When I woke up, for a minute I thought I was the victim of a delusion. But there she was in the dining room. Dressed in her green work coat, which I did not remember she wore before, elbows on my working table, Nené was sipping a cup of tea.

'Have a cup of tea, Carlitos. I was on my way out. I have to open the shop. Don't you have any more crackers? There's nothing to eat here, you are going to starve. This girl here with you, who is she?'

She pointed to a metal frame with a photo of Elsa Martinez and I covered up to our ears on a very cold day on the promenade in Mar del Plata. Before I had a chance to decide what to answer, she continued.

'She has a certain air of an evil bird, some kind of a falcon, right'

This is only a half truth. Elsa Martinez has a big nose but she is not evil, not at all.

'I don't think you will end up marrying her, it is not to your advantage. She is a calculating self interested woman.'

Outraged at the unfair attack, I chose to remain silent.

Suddenly, as if on an impulse, Nené picked up the phone and dialled a number. She started a conversation with a certain Beba, whom, as I could ascertain by the conversation, was her colleague. That is to say, the owner of another veterinary in the district of Flores. They talked about business, about something that had happened at Nazca and Avellaneda, about products and prices, and at a given moment, Nené said,

'I was finally able to have two orgasms as one is supposed to. I'll tell you all about it on Saturday.'

Suddenly, she was in front of my mirror in the bathroom, sticking her fingers into her eyes.

'I use contacts. I was fed up with conventional glasses. They make you look old, and I still hope I'll get married and have children.'

I had already calmed down, so I judged impartially. She was really an ugly woman, big hips, narrow shoulders and flabby titties, worth nothing. Her features were somewhat violent, rather masculine, and she had a coarse complexion. How and under what need did I descend to make love to her?

'A small example will suffice,' she said, as if she had read my mind. 'I know you are never going back to the veterinary and I do not want you to come by, either.'

That was the last thing she said. She closed the door, and a second later I heard the sound of the elevator.

Somehow, I felt that my home and I were contaminated by Nené's intrusion. I experienced a violent revolting sensation and went on a sort of a disinfection exercise. I stood up the mattress to air out against a wall, I changed the linen on my bed, I washed up all the dishes we had used including the tea-cup and saucer Nené had used. I cleaned the tabletop with a dishcloth and I mopped the floor. I then took a long, long bath.

6. Waiting for an outcome

We haven't heard about the rotten potatoes or the glass balls. We know nothing about Nené and her designs.

I tried to go on with my everyday life.

One day, I noticed that my dog-eared *Appleton* was missing

all the pages with the number three as the last digit. Another day, I found a notebook page with a clumsy childish drawing representing a small house with an A frame roof and a tree with a round top.

Once, they took all the buttons from my raincoat but left me a Rolex watch. I was the winner here. The next time they stole the eight volumes of my classic edition of *Don Quixote*, the Spanish Classics edition, annotated by Francisco Rodríguez Marin. Instead, they left a paper fan with some kind of advertising for a Japanese Cleaners located at Lomas de Zamora. This time, I was the loser.

Thus, as the days went by, the pillages and the offerings continued to multiply. I did not like this situation. All those robberies and destruction hurt me, always falling upon things I had personally bought, all very dear to me. And I was not interested in the presents left behind even if sometimes they had material value, for I had not desired them.

All these interchanges were happening in the midst of absolute triviality. There was nothing unusual they could take from me. And they never left something unusual for me. I never received an object from another planet, a magic idol or prodigious talisman, a mummy finger, a pterodactyl bone. No. I only received very common twentieth century objects. What am I saying, twentieth century? Just the last decade. Sometimes, they were new and came in their original package, sometimes they were used and sometimes they were broken.

At the beginning, I systematically threw all presents in the trash bin. But, when I saw that sooner or later they would unfailingly return, I left them where they showed up, without ever touching them.

Thus, my otherwise tidy and organized apartment at the end of Villa Urquiza became a senseless storage room. And then one day I could no longer distinguish my original belongings from those which showed up as presents.

This process took a few months, and I had already resigned myself to living as best as I could.

Nonetheless, I can now say that for the last month or so my visitors seem to have forgotten me. In vain, I check the tangle of anarchic stuff on a daily basis but I realize they are always the same. There are no additions or subtractions. Or that, at least, is what I believe.

If things continue like this, that is if I am ever sure that I have been forgotten forever, perhaps I will decide to restore my house and my life. As in the good old times when I had attained a certain order and had been able to take care of myself.

But perhaps I am just facing a truce. So, for the time being, I prefer to wait a while longer. And see what happens.

A LIFESTYLE

In my youth before becoming a farmer and cattle-raiser, I was an employee of the Council. Things happened this way:

I was twenty-four years old at the time and had no close relatives. I was living in this same small flat on Santa Fe Avenue between Canning y Aráoz Streets.

It is well known that even within such a reduced space accidents can occur. In my case, it was a tiny accident: when I tried to open the door to go to work my key broke off in the lock.

After having vainly attempted to make use of screwdrivers and hooks, I decided to call a locksmith's shop. While I waited for the locksmith, I phoned the Council to tell them I would be late.

Luckily, the locksmith came quite promptly. About this man, I can only remember that he was young but that his hair was extremely white. I spoke to him through the spyhole:

'The key broke up inside the lock.'

He made a slight gesture of annoyance.

'Inside? In that case, it's going to be more difficult. I will have to work for at least three hours and I will have to charge you about...'

He quoted a very high sum.

'I haven't got that much money at home,' I replied, 'but as soon as I am out, I will go to the bank in the corner and I can pay you.'

He looked at me as if reproaching me, as if I had proposed something immoral:

'I am very sorry, sir,' he stated with an exemplary courtesy, 'but I am not only a member of the Argentinean Locksmiths Union but also one of the main writers of our institution's

Magna Carta. No point has been left to chance in it. Were you to have the pleasure of reading this exciting document, you would learn in the chapter dedicated to the 'Basic Apothegms' that the perfect locksmith is not allowed to collect his fee after having done the job.'

Incredulous, I smiled:

'You must be pulling my leg.'

'My dear sir, the subject of the Magna Carta of our Argentinean Locksmiths Union is too serious to be joking about it. Long years of intensive study led us to write our Magna Carta in which no detail has been neglected and where a moral principle rules its various chapters. Of course, not everyone can understand them as we often use a symbolic or esoteric language. Nevertheless, I think you will understand verse 7 of our Introduction: 'Gold will open the doors, and the doors will worship it.'

I was not going to listen to such nonsense:

'Please,' I told him, 'be reasonable. Open my door and I will pay you immediately.'

'I am sorry sir, every profession has its own ethical rules, and the locksmiths' are quite strict. Have a good day, sir.'

And he was gone.

For a moment, I felt confused. I phoned the Council again and told them I probably would not be able to go to work that day. I then thought about the white-haired locksmith and said to myself, 'This is a madman. I'll call another locksmith and, just in case, I won't tell them I haven't any cash until they have opened my door.'

I searched in the phone book and I made my call.

'What is the address?' asked a circumspect feminine voice.

'Santa Fe 3653, 10th A.'

She hesitated a moment, asked me to repeat the address and said:

'Impossible, sir, the Argentinean Locksmiths Union's

Magna Carta forbids doing any work in those premises.'

A great wave of anger swept over me: 'But, listen! Don't be so fool...!'

Without waiting for me to finish, she cut me off.

I returned to the phonebook and made as many as twenty calls to other locksmiths. All of them flatly refused to do the job as soon as they learned of my address.

'Very well,' I thought, 'I shall find the solution elsewhere.'

I called the building's caretaker and I described my problem.

'There are two things. First, I don't know how to open locks. Second, even if I knew how, I wouldn't do it. My job is to do the cleaning, not smelling rats. Besides, you have never been too generous with your tips.'

I began to feel nervous and performed a series of useless illogical actions. I had a cup of coffee, smoked a cigarette, sat down, stood up, took some steps, washed my hands and drank a glass of water...

Then I remembered Mónica Di Chiave. I dialled, waited and heard her voice.

'Mónica,' I said to her, adopting a mellow and nonchalant tone of voice, 'How are you doing? How are things with you, beautiful?'

Her answer astounded me.

'Now you remember to call? It´s obvious you must be very much in love... Haven't seen any traces of you for around fifteen days.'

Arguing with an angry woman is something beyond my strength, especially in the mentally diminished situation I was in at that moment. Nevertheless, I tried to explain quickly what was happening to me. I do not know if she did not understand me or would not listen to me. The last thing she said before hanging up was:

'I am nobody's toy.'

I had to do a second series of useless illogical actions.

I then called the Council again, hoping that some co-worker could come and open my door. Bad luck, I had to talk to Enzo Paredes whom I detested for being stupid and a joker.

'So you can't leave your house?' was his loathsome answer. 'You don't know what else to invent for not coming to work!'

Something close to a homicidal urge took hold of me. I hung up, called again and asked to be put through to Miguel Ángel Laporta who was a little less thick. He seemed interested in finding a solution.

'Tell me, what got broken, was it the key or the lock?'

'The key.'

'And did it stay inside the lock?'

'One half stayed inside,' I replied, now somewhat exasperated by the questioning, 'and the other is outside.'

'Didn't you try with a screwdriver, pulling out the bit inside?'

'Yes, of course I tried but it's impossible.'

'Oh, well, you are going to have to call a locksmith.'

'I already called,' I answered while trying to suppress the anger that was choking me, 'but they want me to pay in advance.'

'Well, just pay them, end of story.'

'But I haven't any cash with me.'

Then he got annoyed:

'Well, skinny, you have all kinds of problems.'

I could not find a quick reply. I should have asked him to lend me some money but his phrase was the last straw, and I could not think straight.

So I wasted the rest of the day.

Next morning, I had an early rise and began to make new calls. But, something rather frequent, I found that the phone was out of order. An insoluble problem: How to phone to get help, not having a phone?

I went out onto the balcony and started to shout to the people passing by Avenida Santa Fe. The noise in the street was deafening. Who could hear anyone shouting from a tenth floor? The one or two people who did casually raised their heads and continued on their way.

I then had an idea: I placed five sheets of paper and four carbon papers in a typewriter and wrote the following message: 'Sir or Madam, the key to my front door got broken inside the lock. I have been locked in for two days. Please do something to free me. Santa Fe 3653, 10° A.' I threw the five sheets from the balcony. From such a height, the possibilities of the sheets dropping vertically were minimal. Carried by the whim of the wind, they fluttered haphazardly. Three fell on the road and immediately were run over and blackened by the incessant flow of vehicles. Another landed on a shop awning but the fifth one fell on the pavement.

Immediately, a diminutive gentleman picked it up and read it. He then looked up, shading his eyes with his left hand. I made a friendly gesture to call his attention. He tore the paper up in many tiny pieces and, with an angry gesture, threw them into the gutter.

To be brief, during many weeks I continued making all sort of attempts. I threw hundreds of messages from the balcony. Either they were not read or they were but were not taken seriously.

One day, I saw an envelope that had been slipped under the door of my flat. It was a warning from the telephone company. My phone would be cut off for non-payment. Soon, in succession, the gas, electricity and water were also cut off.

At first, I consumed my provisions in an irrational manner but, in time, I realised that such behaviour was a mistake.

I placed some containers in the balcony to collect the rainwater. I ripped out the useless ornamental plants and in their pots planted tomatoes, lettuce, lentils and other vegetables which I tend with much love and care. I also require animal proteins, so I learned to breed and reproduce in captivity insects, spiders and rodents. Sometimes, I catch some sparrow or pigeon.

On sunny days, I manage, using a magnifying glass and a piece of paper, to light a fire. For fuel, I gradually burned the books, pieces of furniture and the floor planks. I discovered that there are always in every house more things than are necessary.

I live comfortably, although lacking a few things I do not know what is happening in other places, I do not read the papers and I can no longer operate my television or radio.

From my balcony, I watch the outside world and I notice some changes. One day, the trams stopped circulating. On another occasion, Santa Fe Avenue, which was a two-way street, became a one-way street. I do not know how many years have gone by since these changes took place. I have lost all notion of time but the mirror, my baldness, my long white beard and the pain in my joints all tell me that I am quite old.

My amusement is to let my thoughts wander. I have no fears or ambitions.

In short, I am relatively happy.

AN ENLIGHTENING BOOK

LUDWIG BOITUS: STELZVÖGEL, GOTTINGEN, 1972

In his brief prologue to *Stelzvögel*, Professor Franz Klamm explains that Dr. Ludwig Boitus travelled from Gottingen to Huayllén-Naquén with the sole purpose of studying in situ the assimilative attraction of the long-legged bird popularly known as calegüinas (this name has almost unanimous acceptance in the specialist literature in Spanish and it will be used here). *Stelzvögel* fills an acute gap in our knowledge of the subject. Before Dr. Boitus' exhaustive investigations, the presentation of which takes up almost a third of the volume, little was known for certain about calegüinas. In fact, except for fragmentary qualitative studies by Bulovic, Balbón, Laurencena and others, works plagued by whimsical unsubstantiated claims, before *Stelzvögel* the scientific community lacked a reliable basis on which to base further research. In his work, Dr. Boitus starts from the perhaps debatable premise that the calegüina's main character trait is its very strong personality (using the term personality in the sense established by Fox and his school). This personality is so potent that simply being in the presence of a calegüina is enough to induce, strongly, calegüinas like behaviour in other animals.

The calegüinas are found exclusively in the Huayllén-Naquén lagoon. There, they flourish, some estimates put the population as high as one million, helped both by local by-laws, which make hunting them illegal and by the fact that their flesh is inedible and their feathers have no industrial use. In common with other long legged birds, they feed on fish, Batrachia and the larvæ of mosquitoes and other insects. Although they possess well developed wings, they rarely fly and, when they do, they never go beyond the limits of the lagoon. They are of a similar size to storks, though their beaks are slightly larger, and they do not migrate. Their back and wings are a blueish black, their head, chest and belly, a yellowish white. Their legs are pale yellow. Their habitat, the Huayllén-Naquén lagoon, is shallow but wide. Since there are no bridges across it, in spite of many representations to that end, the locals are obliged to make a long detour in order to get to the opposite side. This has had the effect of making complaints to the local newspaper almost continuous but communication between the shores of the lagoon rather scarce. To the uninformed observer, it would appear that residents could cross the lagoon quickly and easily by using stilts, and, even without them, at its deepest point, the water would barely reach the waist of a man of average height. However, the locals know, although perhaps in an intuitive way only, the assimilative power of the calegüinas, and the fact is that they prefer not to attempt the crossing, choosing instead, as already stated, to go around the lagoon, which is encircled by an excellent asphalt road.

All this has not stopped the hiring of stilts to tourists becoming the single most important part of the Huayllén-Naquén economy, a circumstance that is perhaps justifiable in view of the scarcity of basic resources in the region. The absence of serious competition and the lack of official pricing have made the hiring of stilts a very costly business indeed, inflating prices to outrageous levels is the only way tradesmen can recoup their inevitable losses. In fact, there is a rather limited Huayllén-Naquén by-law stipulating that shops hiring stilts should display a sign, positioned in open view and written in bold lettering, warning that the use of stilts may lead to fairly serious psychological alterations. As a rule, tourists tend not to heed these warnings and, for the most part, treat them as a joke. It should be noted that it is simply not possible to make sure that the notices are read by every single tourist even when, as is undeniably the case, the shopkeepers comply with the by-law punctiliously and place the signs in highly conspicuous places. The authorities are notoriously inflexible on this point. It is true that inspections are not very frequent and are always preceded by a warning sent a few minutes beforehand. But, the inspectors are known to perform their duties conscientiously, and it can only be coincidence that there is no recorded case of a shopkeeper being sanctioned under the by-law.

Once in possession of their stilts, the tourists, either by themselves or in cheerful chattering groups of two, three, five or ten go into the Huayllén-Naquén lagoon with the aim of reaching the opposite shore where they can buy, at very reasonable prices, tins of exquisite fish, a product that provides the main source of income for the population on that side of the lagoon. For the first two or three hundred metres, the tourists advance happily, laughing, shouting, playing practical jokes and frightening the caleguinas, which, like all long-legged birds, are extremely nervous creatures. Gradually, as they penetrate deeper and deeper into the lagoon, the tourists become more subdued while, metre by metre, the density of caleguinas increases. Soon the birds are so numerous that progress becomes extremely difficult for the tourists. The caleguinas no longer run or fly away nervously, as their numbers rise they appear to grow in confidence although their behaviour could also be explained by the fact that, by then, most movement is physically impossible. Whatever the reason, there comes a moment when shouting is no longer enough and it becomes necessary to use sticks and hands to shoo the calegüinas out of the way. Even then, they concede very little ground. This is generally the moment when the tourists fall silent and the joking and laughing comes to an end. Then, and only then, they notice a dense humming emanating from the throats of the thousands of calegüinas, filling the entire lagoon. In its timbre, this humming is not very different from that of doves; it is, however, considerably more intense. It enters the ears of the tourists and resonates inside their heads, it fills their minds so completely that, gradually, they too begin to hum. To start with, this humming is a poor imitation of the birds but soon it becomes impossible to distinguish between the humming of the humans and that of the calegüinas. At this point, the tourists often start to experience a choking sensation, they can detect nothing but calegüinas for as far as the eye can see and soon lose the ability to differentiate between land and the water of the lagoon. In front and behind, left and right, they see an endlessly repeating monotonous desert of black and white made up of wings, beaks and feathers. There is usually one tourist, especially if there is a large group of them on the lagoon, who perceives the wisdom and convenience of returning to Huayllén-Naquén and sacrificing their prospective purchase of exquisite fish at very reasonable prices from the opposite shore.

But where is the opposite shore? How can they go back if they have lost all notion of the direction they came from? How can they go back if there are no longer any points of reference, if everything is black and white, an endlessly repeating landscape of wings, beaks and feathers? And eyes: two million blinking expressionless eyes. In spite of all the evidence that returning is no longer an option, the tourist who is most lucid or, rather, least delirious, addresses his companions with some pathetic exhortation. 'Friends, let us go back the way we came!' But his companions cannot understand his strident croaks; so different are they from the gentle humming they are now accustomed to. At this point, even though they themselves answer with the same unintelligible croaks, deep down they are still conscious of the fact that they are human. Fear, however, has unhinged them, and they all begin to croak simultaneously. Unfortunately, this chorus of croaks has no meaningful content and, even if they wanted to, the tourists would be unable to communicate their final coherent thought, that they are all calegüinas. It is then that the elders of the calegüinas community, who up to this point have kept knowingly silent, begin to croak with all their might. It is a triumphant croak, a cry of victory that starts from that inner circle and spreads quickly and tumultuously through the length and breadth of the Huayllén-Naquén lagoon and beyond its limits to the remotest houses of the nearby town. The locals put their fingers in their ears and smile. Happily, the noise lasts barely five minutes, and only after it has completely stopped do the tradesmen get back to making as many pairs of stilts as tourists have entered the lagoon.

A QUESTION OF AGE

On those rainy days, Mario would insist on having some of Grandma's special sugar coated fritters. Flattered and smiling and only too happy to comply, she'd send Coca to reorganize the junk room or to rid the closets of dust balls. This is how she managed to have the kitchen to herself.

In that great dark solitary house, I could choose to stick around, as Grandma's veined hands ever so slowly fashioned her 'frittahs,' or go with Coca and watch her redo the junk room. Coca called it the *attic* but I knew very well from my illustrated dictionary that an attic couldn't be a ground floor cubbyhole looking out on a brick boundary wall. This end of the yard was quiet and moist with an old rectangle of rusted iron, some flowery tiles and a faucet for watering the garden. Although the faucet had no spigot, and, in any case, no one watered the garden. In fact, it was hardly a garden at all. It had no plants or cultivated flowers, just an assortment of weeds and vines along with pill bugs, ants, ponds, toads and mice.

I think I was fourteen before I discovered what the outside of the house looked like. I hardly ever went out and, when I did, I always came and went using the sidewalk on our side of the street, so I knew the houses across the street by heart but not the one that had sheltered me since I was born. One day, I decided not to make any diagonal crossings just right angles. From the corner, I walked along the sidewalk opposite our house. To my left, loomed wire or wrought iron fences and overgrown plants, to my right, trees imprisoned every few meters in dirt squares. Their cool restless branches would link up overhead in spring and summer, sifting the sun's rays.

But this was a winter day, and dusk had set in. Everything was so sad, the breeze mute and listless, the street empty, the lights dying in high ceilinged rooms. I don't know why, they made me want to cry, and suddenly I thought of Mirta, an older girl who went to my school. I was standing on blue and white mosaic tiles consisting of nine little squares each, and the wind was about to carry off a dirty page from *El Gráfico*. I stepped on it in time and, without bending over, read, *'Musimessi, star goalkeeper for Newell's Old Boys.'* I let it go, and the paper groaned harshly as it scudded along before ending up in the sewer.

How gloomy my house was! You could hardly see it. Dark withered vines covered the rusty black iron grille. Behind it, grey palms, peeling pines and the almighty rubber plant obscured even the dim outline of our house whose cracked and stained walls resembled nothing so much as roadmaps. But the gabled roof, its once-red tiles now a muddy violet, stood out in sharp relief against the white sky.

The house also had an attic but since Coca slept there it was no longer an attic but a *bedroom*. Grandma, of course, called it the *maid's room* (just as streetcars for her were *trolleys*, shoes *slippers* and the Primera Junta subway line forever *The Anglo*). I liked the little room with its upside down V for a ceiling and its thick beams of dark wood. Every night, Coca would listen to the radio play broadcast by Radio El Mundo on a very old, very tall and very hard to hear radio that towered above a kitchen bench. Half the room was taken up by a huge three door mahogany wardrobe with an oval mirror. Inside its doors, hung tango singer, Carlos Gardel, in sky blue gaucho garb, cowboy actor, Robert Taylor, and dapper movie idol, Ángel Magaña, in coat and bowtie. There were also posters of the Virgin of Luján and of the saintly Mapuche Indian boy and smooth Ceferino Namuncurá. On the wall, a colour photo taken the day of her wedding to Ricardo showed a different

Coca with her hair piled high, her lips red. A bottle of cologne and a sulfur stick sat on the marble topped lamp table. The best thing in the room, however, was a window like a porthole with two pink panes that could be opened one at a time.

And so when Coca said she was going to clean the attic it was understood she meant the junk room. And if it pleased Grandma to make fritters for Mario, it was not so much that she liked doing it but that she could regain a little of her former importance when it was she who ran the house, when they had not yet put her on the sidelines. Of course, since she was senile (arteriosclerosis, eighty six years old), her manias and confusion came as no surprise. She could not be blamed for lying or making things up sometimes. Dr. Calvino explained that such maladies were typical of old age and, since there was no cure, it was best just to accept the situation. In any case, Grandma was adorable and didn't bother anybody.

She would pass autumn and winter afternoons with a shawl across her knees and a scarf around her shoulders, rocking away in an enormous chair that yet seemed lost amid the endless lilac coloured flowers and greenish birds on the living room walls. Sitting there with her hands intertwined, she would think about who knows what, looking out past the black oval table with its crude crocheted doily. Or she would polish all the metal objects in the house till they shone scandalously in the midst of things so dull and melancholy. I used to bring her bronze candelabra or silver fruit bowls but Mario put his foot down, saying I was only encouraging her tendency toward what might be called obsession.

Be that as it may, now that the weather was milder, Grandma had taken to wandering about in the yard's many unexplored corners. In the evening, she would sit well away from the house on a little straw chair until, at length, Coca would fetch her back inside, citing the dangers of the evening dew. Convincing Grandma to stay in the living room was not easy, however, and every day she spent more time in the garden usually near the ruined statue. Dr. Calvino advised us to let her have her way so long as she did not catch cold given the weak state of her bronchial tubes.

When Mario got up to secure the shutters the night of the Santa Rosa storm he was shocked to see Grandma out in the rain, a fragile plant being blown about by the raging icy wind. Dr. Calvino diagnosed pneumonia, and now to senility was added delirium. Grandma started seeing little men. 'Little men?' Right, the little men in yellow shorts and red jackets with tall black boots on their feet and blue velvet caps on their heads. It was no good interrupting her with the news that Telma had given birth to twins or showing her the sheets Aunt Marcelina had just finished embroidering. The city of little men was called Natania and consisted mainly of woods, towers and bridges. The fortress of the king and his three ministers was guarded by winged lions and eagle headed bulls. 'By statues of lions and bulls?' No, by flesh and blood lions and bulls.

Dr. Calvino put on the special face that family doctors will assume, and the house became an obligatory stop for commiserating cousins, however distant. When finally the old lady's delicate little life expired completely the undertakers showed up with the absurd trappings of death. They set up a funeral chapel in the room where Grandma used to polish her metals, and the coffin handles shone as if she had buffed them herself. The aunts, one of whom was still single, recalled how as a young girl Grandma was always ready and willing to work, while the uncles, notaries and lawyers all sipped coffee and cognac and weighed the chances of Balbín-Frondizi versus Perón-Quijano in the upcoming presidential elections.

I passed the night viewing a procession of faces (with an occasional thought for Mirta) until, deserting the wake, I took refuge in the garden's thick tangle of plants, surrounded by scraggy palms and blue bellflowers that died almost as soon as they were plucked. Remembering her there, with her glasses and her black coat, I cried, though quietly.

Since Grandma was no longer around to be scandalized, Mario allowed a so called fiancé to move in with Coca (now separated from the Ricardo in the colour photo). He turned out to be a grim sort with little hair, bad manners and no words. During the first week, returning from I don't know where and always at about the same time of day, he would spend the afternoons gazing out the round window at the house opposite ours. Saturday, he showed a perversely creative streak. Things were just fine as they were but, with Mario's consent, he embarked on a brutal revolution.

He planned to start with the yard, no less, cutting down weeds, sowing grass, cultivating flowers. And then the garden would be nothing more than a garden, smooth and clear and clean. No longer would I be able to think and play in secret mysterious places. No longer could I go where the fattest palm, the wild privet hedge and the fallen statue covered in moss and lichen (as my eighth grade botany text would say) formed a private space.

The statue's base was completely hidden by weeds but below it, if someone were able to lift the heavy thing, the ground was flat and compacted to form a perfect circle. That's where we first began to communicate. The block of marble had been lost in the garden for some time now. A half blurred little heart and arrow read Elisa and Mario yet Mario had been a widower for more than twenty years.

A neighbourhood dog delayed the garden takeover. Barking and whining day and night, it was a stupid unbearable dog, and, indeed, the boyfriend couldn't bear it. In a gesture typical of the way he went about solving problems, he tossed some poisoned meat over the dividing wall. The neighbours, who for other reasons were just as boorish, filed a complaint with the police, and he had to spend two days in jail.

Once free, he turned his attention to redoing the inside of the house. Mario was already very old and quite powerless, one more useless thing that, instead of finding a niche in the junk room, was found in the library. With careful old fashioned penmanship, he sat copying, why? what for?, romantic high-sounding poems in a schoolboy's notebook. But the weeks flew by, and the guy had almost finished remodelling and painting the whole house in ever brighter colours. He would soon be attacking the garden.

He began to clear it, moving in a circle that centred on the house. Of course, there was a good way to go before he reached the statue so I still had time to talk and get more details. Meanwhile, he pulled up the first weeds, got rid of the cans and rocks that had accumulated over more than twenty five years of idleness, killed countless innocent toads and thus completed the first round of the circle. Fortunately, since each new round covered a larger area, his progress became slower by the day.

At school, I was extremely nervous, imagining that he was closing in on Julio, the pine tree, (when looked at from the proper angle, the knots read Julio) and, indeed, he had done so. The ground was completely cleared and smoothed down around it. They had already begun an orderly migration and, even though they should have let me know, they never told me where they would settle next. To make matters worse, he passed up his regular Sunday session with the boys, those pool hall clowns with cigarettes hanging from their mouths, and stayed in the garden drinking maté with Coca and reading lies in the newspaper, so I could make little progress. The next day I had a zoology test but my eyes kept gravitating toward the window, making it impossible to concentrate. I wasn't in a mood for amoebas and paramecia, I couldn't think about such stupidities, knowing without a doubt that Monday he would get around to the pedestal.

I went to say goodbye at two in the morning and became so upset I couldn't sleep a wink. Zoology was the last thing on my mind. I tried cheating but the teacher caught me and took away my test. At last, sitting there on the school bench in peace and comfort, I was able to recall once more the little men in yellow shorts and red jackets with tall black boots on their feet and blue velvet caps on their heads.

CHASTISEMENT
BY THE LAMBS

According to very diverse and always very reliable sources, the 'Chastisement by the Lambs' is becoming increasingly common in several parts of Buenos Aires and the surrounding area.

All reports agree in their description of the Chastisement; suddenly, fifty white lambs appear, you could say 'out of the blue,' and immediately charge towards their victim, obviously chosen beforehand. In a few short seconds, they devour the person, leaving only a skeleton. As suddenly as they arrived, they then disperse and pity anyone who tries to block their escape! Many fatal cases were recorded early on before prospective heroes learned from the fate of their predecessors. These days, no one dares oppose the Chastisement.

There is little point in going into the details of the phenomenon, everybody is largely aware of the facts thanks to the media, and photographic and video documentation is widely available. Nevertheless, the majority of people are worried by the Chastisement and its consequences. The majority of people, however, are simple, they lack education and the power of reflection and their concern is limited to a desire that the Chastisement does not exist. Of course, this desire does not put an end to the Chastisement and certainly does not help to determine its causes or raison d'être.

These people's basic mistake is that, as immersed as they are in the facts of the Chastisement itself, they have forgotten the victims. During, say, the first one hundred executions, what kept me awake at night was the irrefutable existence of lambs that were not only carnivores but predators, and of human flesh at that. Later, however, I observed that, by concentrating on those details, I had been neglecting something essential, the victim's personality.

So I began investigating the lives of the deceased. Borrowing my methodology from sociologists, I started with the most elementary, the socio-economic data. Statistics turned out to be useless; the victims came from all social and economic strata.

I decided to change the focus of my investigation. I searched for friends and relatives and eventually managed to extract the pertinent information from them. Their statements were varied and sometimes contradictory but gradually I began to hear a certain type of phrase more and more frequently: 'Let the poor man rest in peace, but the truth is that …'

I had a sudden and almost irresistible insight into the situation and was almost completely sure of my germinal hypothesis the day the Chastising Lambs devoured my prosperous neighbour, Dr. P.R.V., the same person in whose office, but I will come to that.

In an absolutely natural way, P.R.V.'s case led me to the definitive understanding of the enigma.

The truth is I hated Nefario and, while I would not want the base passion of my hate to pollute the cold objectivity of this report, nonetheless, in order to provide a full explanation of the phenomenon, I feel obliged to allow myself a digression of a personal nature. Although it may not interest anyone, this diversion is essential, as long as I am believed, for people to judge the veracity of my hypothesis concerning the conditions necessary to trigger the Chastisement by the Lambs.

Here is the digression.

The fact is the climax of the Chastisement coincided with a lugubrious period in my life. Troubled by poverty, by disorientation, by grief, I felt I was at the bottom of a deep dark well and incapable of imagining any way out. That is how I felt.

Nefario meanwhile, well, as they say, life smiled at him and naturally so since the only objective of his wicked existence was money. That was his only concern, earning money, money for itself, and toward this holy purpose he concentrated all his merciless energy without regard for others. Needless to say, he was overwhelmingly successful. Nefario truly was what you would call a 'winner.'

At that time, I have already said this, I found myself in a very needy situation. It is so easy to take advantage of anyone who is suffering! Nefario, that greedy vulture who had never read a book, was an editor. For want of better things to do, I used to undertake some translation and proof-reading jobs for him. Nefario not only paid me a pittance but also took pleasure in humiliating me with excuses and delays.

(Suffering abuse and failure was already part of my persona, and I was resigned to them.)

When I delivered to him my latest batch of work, an awkward and hideous translation, Nefario, as on so many other occasions, said to me, 'Unfortunately, I am unable to pay you today, haven't got a penny.'

He told me this while in his lavish office, well dressed, smelling of perfume and with a smile on his face and, of course, as a 'winner'. I thought of my cracked shoes, my worn clothes, my family's urgent needs and my burden of pain. With effort, I said, 'And when do you think?'

'Let's do this,' his tone was optimistic and protective, as if he were trying to help me. 'I can't do this Saturday because I am taking a short break on the Rio beaches. But the following one around eleven in the morning, come to my house, and we will settle this little account.' He shook my hand cordially and gave me a friendly and encouraging pat on the shoulder. A fortnight went by. The yearned for Saturday arrived, and so did I at the beautiful 11 de Septiembre Street. The green of the trees, the smell of vegetation, the radiance of the sky and the beauty of the district, all made me feel even more desolate. At five past eleven, I rang the bell.

'The master is resting,' I was told by a maid in uniform.

I hesitated a moment and said, 'And the lady of the house?'

'Who is it, Rosa?' I heard someone ask.

'It's me, madam.' I raised my voice, clinging to the possibility. 'Is Mister Nefario at home?' Rosa went inside, and was replaced by the cosmetic-covered face of Nefario's wife. In a tone that reminded me of a heavy cigar smoking tycoon, she enquired, 'Haven't you been told that the master is taking his rest?'

'Yes, madam, but we had an appointment at eleven'

'Yes but he is resting just now,' she replied in an unappealable manner.

'Might he have left something for me?' I asked stupidly, as if I did not know Nefario!

'No.'

'But we had an appointment at ...'

'I am telling you, he did not leave anything, sir. Please don't be annoying, sir.'

At that moment, I heard a jabbering bleating sound and witnessed the arrival of the Chastisement by the Lambs. I moved to one side and, so as to be more secure, climbed the fence although my conscience told me that the Chastisement was not searching for me. Like a tornado, the lambs burst into the front garden and, before the last ones could arrive, those in the lead were already inside the house.

In a few seconds, like a drain swallowing water from a sink, Nefario's door absorbed all the animals, leaving the garden trampled, the plants destroyed.

Through an exquisitely designed window, Mrs. Nefario appeared,

'Come, sir, come!' she pleaded tearfully, her face congested. 'Please help us, sir!'

Out of a certain sense of curiosity, I went in. I saw the furniture overturned, mirrors broken. I could not see the lambs.

'They are upstairs!' I was informed by Mrs. Nefario as she pulled me in the direction of the danger. 'They are in our room! Do something, don't be a coward, behave like a man!'

I managed to resist, firmly. Nothing could be more against my principles than to oppose the Chastisement by the Lambs. A confused cacophony of hooves could be heard coming from upstairs. The round woolly backs could be seen shaking happily, accompanied by some forceful movements aimed at an unseen object within the mass. For one fleeting moment, I perceived Nefario, it was only for a second; dishevelled and horrified, he shouted something and tried to attack the lambs with a chair. However, he soon sunk into the white curly wools like someone violently swallowed by quicksand. There was another centrical commotion and the growing noise of jaws tearing and crushing and, every now and then, the thin sharp noise of a bone being cracked. Their first withdrawal manoeuvres told me that the lambs had accomplished their task, and, soon after, the little animals started their swift descent of the stairs. I could see some bloodstains in the otherwise unpolluted whiteness of their wool.

Curiously, that blood, to me a symbol of ethical affirmation, caused Mrs. Nefario to lose all reason. Still addressing me with tearful insults and telling me that I was a coward, she erupted in the living room with a large knife in her hands. As I knew very well the fate of those who attempted to obstruct the Chastisement by the Lambs, I respectfully remained in the background while observing the short and remarkable spectacle of the dismemberment and ingestion of Mrs. Nefario. Afterwards, the fifty lambs reached 11 de Septiembre Street and, as on many other occasions, they escaped by dispersing into the city.

Rosa, I do not know why, seemed a little impressed. I called out a few comforting words to her before, free of hate, saying goodbye to the girl with a smile.

It is true, I had not and would not manage to obtain from Nefario the payment for that awkward and hideous translation. Nevertheless, the green of the trees, the smell of vegetation, the radiance of the sky and the beauty of the district filled my heart with joy. I started to sing.

I knew then that the dark well into which I had sunk was beginning to be lit up with the first rays of hope.

DOCTOR MOREAU
DID IT

1

Everything in life has its season. And so the day came when Marina said, 'I want you to meet my folks.'

2

Ten years have passed since that muggy summer afternoon out in Acassuso. I can still see the eucalyptus trees swaying overhead and smell the distant rain. It's Marina's face I can't remember.

She was a knockout, I'm sure of that. I was in love with her, of course, but no one can deny she was a knockout. And what else, what else can I remember? She was a tall brunette, dumb and cheerful, infinitely loveable. How many times we swore we were meant for each other! I wonder if I seem as hazy to her now as she does to me.

3

We were in our twenties, and everything was going right for me. Till then, I'd never known bad luck and, if I had, I'd forgotten it. With wide-eyed optimism, I took for granted the honesty of politicians, the promotions I'd earn during my career, the completion of my studies and the dignity of mankind. I inhabited the best of all possible worlds.

Except for minor foreseeable blips, my plans were all on target. There was no doubt that within a year at most Marina and I would wed.

So, as everything in life has its season, the day came when Marina said, 'I want you to meet my folks.'

4

Señora Stella Maris was an older version of Marina (whose whole name was, unfortunately, Marina Ondina). I expected Marina to be just like her in another twenty years when we'd have a daughter of our own with names less cloying. Such was the long-range goal I had in mind as I said hello. Señora Stella Maris was, of course, an elegant lady of forty-five, tall, brunette and cheerful.

Marina's father, on the other hand, turned out to be the most disgusting man I've ever known. His lot in life was to be short. Now this is not a serious problem. He was not a dwarf, he just wasn't very tall. What completely floored me was the fact that his head alone took up more that half his height. And, my God, what a head! The first thing that caught my attention (or, rather, put me off) was his strange colour. His skin, reflecting the shifting light, could be dazzling at times, varying from pink to black with all the shades in between. At the same time, it seemed clammy and sticky. He was completely bald and clearly always had been. No hair would ever sprout on that head. Its upper half threatened to become a perfect globe but, foiled at the equator (more or less at the height of his missing ears), the head morphed into a cylindrical column which, without any transition for neck or shoulders, became lost among the folds of a kind of yellow floor length terry cloth tunic. In other words, Marina's father had the same diameter from top to bottom. He was a round topped monolith, wrapped half way up with a yellow towel. Located a few centimetres above the toga, Señor Octavio's mouth, a mobile toothless fissure at once supple and hard as horn, would draw in until it disappeared or would open so wide it seemed his throat had been slit, and his head, left to teeter on its precarious base by the slipshod assassin, seemed likely to come crashing down at the slightest movement. Where his ears and nose should have been, the skin was as polished and smooth as his bald pate, nothing, not even a scar or a wrinkle, not the slightest mark. The two eyes were huge, round and bloodshot with no eyebrows or eyelashes, no whites, no pupils, no expression.

5

'Señor Octavio is on a diet,' explained Señora Stella Maris, seeing me stare at the plate intended for her husband.

Señora Stella Maris, Marina and I ate what you might call normal food. Señor Octavio's plate, on the other hand, was like an anthology of sea life. The sudden stench exploded in my nostrils, bringing tears to my eyes. Since my future father-in-law's sleeves were knotted at the ends, he wielded his knife and fork like a person who'd forgotten to remove his gloves. Round after round of raw fish, molluscs and crustaceans were quickly polished off. By my estimate, he ate at least five kilos of the gaudy things. I could make out squid, shrimp, oysters, crabs, snails, jellyfish, mussels, clams, starfish, sea urchins, coral, sponges and fish of questionable identity.

'Señor Octavio is on a diet,' repeated Señora Stella Maris toward the end of the meal. 'Shall we have our coffee in the living room?'

I made way for Señor Octavio and watched him walk by. He moved erratically, sometimes taking a very quick step, sometimes a very slow one, without the regularity of a limp. His way of walking made me think of a car with four different wheels, triangular, oblong, round and oval. I already mentioned that his yellow toga covered him completely except for his head. The garment's tail was so long it dragged behind him like a bridal train.

Señora Stella Maris placed a tray of cups on an elaborate eight sided coffee table flanked by two small sofas. Marina and I sat in one of them; facing us, with the table in between, sat Señor Octavio and his wife. I now noticed another oddity. As if to emphasize important points when he spoke, invisible arms seemed in motion beneath Señor Octavio's tunic. So violent and frequent were the yellow bubbles formed by the toga, his body appeared to be boiling.

Señor Octavio hogged the conversation. He talked and talked and talked. I wasn't really listening, however. I was asking myself, 'Could this monster possibly be the father of Marina, my lovely delightful angelic Marina?' Suddenly, I was sure that in her youth Señora Stella Maris had been unfaithful to her husband and that Marina was the fruit of an illicit love affair. Carried away by this idea, I found myself casting complicitous looks at Señora Stella Maris, (fortunately, she didn't see them), as if to say I was in on her secret but wasn't about to give her away. On the contrary, I approved wholeheartedly and, in fact, would have forgiven anything rather than acknowledge this babbling monster as the father of my Marina.

A question aimed my way brought me back to the present. The conversation had sunk to a new low with Señora Stella Maris holding forth energetically on the topic of illnesses, one she seemed right at home with.

'You're like a fish in water,' remarked Señor Octavio.

Smiling proudly, she plunged ahead. Her résumé was impressive—operations, fractures, heart attacks, liver ailments, nervous breakdowns. Being somewhat timid, I'd kept quiet up to now but, stung by a look from Marina, I humbly offered up the asthma attacks that plagued me from time to time.

'For asthma,' said Señor Octavio, his voice bubbling over, 'there's nothing better than the sea. The sea is far better than any of those worthless cures doctors prescribe except, of course, for cod liver oil.'

'Really, Octavio,' retorted his wife, 'you can't be serious. Remember that time in Mar del Plata, I caught a cold that lasted two months.'

'Stop fishing for arguments,' Señor Octavio insisted. 'You caught that cold here just a few kilometres from Buenos Aires when we were going to Mar del Plata, not in Mar del Plata. There's nothing like the sea for one's health.'

'Of course, of course,' they said, we said, I said; 'the coastal climate, the iodine, the sand.'

'Nothing better than the sea,' repeated Señor Octavio in a tone of unshakable authority. 'Eight days at sea, and so long asthma! You won't even remember you had it.'

'Sure, Daddy,' agreed Marina, 'you like the sea because you're an Aquarius but there are people who feel out of place in it, me, for example, even though I'm a Pisces.'

'And my sign is Cancer,' said Señora Stella Maris, 'but I don't much like the sea, either.'

'Well, as far as I'm concerned,' Marina confessed, 'it gives me the creeps.'

'Eyewash,' said Señor Octavio. 'It's all a matter of getting the body to adapt. Once you get used to it, you'll see how the sea can soothe your nerves.'

'Talk about nerves,' interrupted Señora Stella Maris, 'what a scare we had on that flight from Río.'

'I warned you.' Señor Octavio's guiding rule of conduct was to argue with whatever was said. 'I told you, go by boat. Boats are safe, comfortable and cheap, you can smell the sea and you can watch the fish. Planes may take less time but there's just no comparison.'

The force with which he said this left us at a loss for words. I didn't feel up to any more conversation. As a matter of fact, I didn't feel up to much at all. Though his high handed pronouncements were delivered with a surprising friendliness, Señor Octavio's monstrous appearance, his watery voice, the smell of his seafood diet, convinced me it was time to go. I could feel the sweat breaking out on my brow, my shirt collar getting tighter. I was quite disoriented, sick in fact, and only wanted to go home. My legs began to sway uncontrollably, and the rumblings in my stomach promised imminent eruption.

But that yapping threesome was unstoppable. Though their comments always met with an objection from Señor Octavio, Señora Stella Maris and Marina did not seem to mind. This was clearly their normal way of conversing.

Once more, I realized that my opinion was being asked for. The topic for debate was where Marina and I should go on our honeymoon. Running her words together without much conviction, Marina suggested the countryside, the hills of Córdoba, the northern provinces; Señor Octavio held firmly for Mar del Plata.

'It's healthier,' he said, 'more natural. You have the sea, the salt, the iodine, the sand, the seashells, nothing better than the sea.'

I was about to pass out. I thought I could hear Marina arguing in favour of somewhere quiet away from the tourists.

'You want somewhere quiet?' Señor Octavio was not to be outdone. 'You've got San Clemente, Santa Clara del Mar, Santa Teresita. There are scores of quiet places on the Atlantic coast!'

With great effort, I got up and announced feebly that it was time to go.

'So early?' asked Señor Octavio, checking his watch. 'It's just eight minutes to midnight.'

The reproach accompanying his words threw me back on the sofa. What a powerful influence that dreadful man exerted!

I clung to the hope that a bottle of whisky recently brought in by Señora Stella Maris might boost my spirits and emptied my glass in one swallow.

'In my heyday,' Señor Octavio was saying, 'when I was young, we would go down to the waterfront bars in Bahía Blanca to dance.'

I was momentarily distracted as I tried to imagine Señor Octavio dancing.

'Sometimes we would dance till the sun came up. But young people these days, eight o'clock and they're already in bed with their wittle wankeypoos and their wittle hot water bottles. Ha, ha, ha! Like a bunch of kindergarten kids.'

Señor Octavio's monologue, punctuated in its final phase by the offensive baby talk, had taken on the unmistakable tone of a personal attack. I stood up, resolved to use force if necessary to get away. Luckily, I didn't have to resort to violence. Señor Octavio recovered his charm and, after holding out the knotted end of his sleeve to me, said, with the unhurried ease of someone preparing to bring a perfect day to a close, 'Well,' and through the terry cloth sleeves he rubbed his hands together, 'now to bed with a good book.'

I nodded vigorously. I wanted to get out of that house. If I'd stayed another second, I believe I would've fainted.

'I'll walk you to the sidewalk,' Marina said.

6

The blessed fragrance of pine and fir trees hit me as we crossed the yard. I breathed deeply, letting the fresh air dispel any lingering fish odours. I felt refreshed, suddenly my stomach trouble was gone.

'You saw poor Daddy?' began Marina.

'Yes,' I answered vaguely, not sure what to say.

'He's much better,' she continued, putting her arm around my waist like someone about to confide a secret. 'A year ago, we couldn't get him out of the pool, day and night in the pool. Now, at least, he eats at the table and sleeps in his bed. That's progress, isn't it?'

She said so many things but I focused on one, the least important: 'Your house has a swimming pool?'

'Of course, didn't I tell you? In the back yard. I can't show it to you now because Daddy's using it. Every night, he takes a dip before he goes to bed. He digests his food better that way.'

I asked a stupid question: 'Doesn't it interfere with his digestion?'

'Oh, no, just the reverse. He needs salt water. True, when he's in the water he gets very aggressive and doesn't recognize anyone, not even us. When he's back on land, well, you saw how nice and friendly he is.'

Appalled and wanting to stall, I checked my watch. Marina was waiting for me to make a move.

'And the neighbours?' I asked. 'Don't they complain?'

'Why should they? There's no noise. Daddy couldn't be any quieter. He doesn't even dive in. He goes to the edge of the pool and let's himself slide in like this, shhhh.'

Her hand slithered softly over my face. Startled, I jumped back. Marina tried to put me at ease with a funny story.

'One night, he was halfway under water near the edge of the pool. Our neighbour's little dog came through the hedge and started sniffing around the pool. Then some of Daddy's arms popped out and shook!'

And with a playful smile, Marina pretended to strangle me. She didn't touch me, she just moved forward with her arms, suddenly strong and rubbery, stretched out in my direction. If before I had jumped backward, I now flew several metres. Marina started laughing, amused by this overreaction. She laughed and laughed and laughed. Her mouth seemed to open all the way to the back of her neck, her head became rounder and longer, her nose and ears disappeared, she lost her magnificent dark hair, and her skin tone was alternating between black and pink. To keep from falling, I leaned against a tree.

'Hey, what's the matter?' Marina shook my arm, and I came to my senses.

She was the same adorable Marina as always, a tall brunette, dumb and cheerful, infinitely loveable.

'It's nothing,' I said, fighting to breathe. 'I just don't feel very good.'

To cheer me up even more, she said, 'Why don't you come over for a swim tomorrow morning. It's Sunday, you know. Bring your suit, and in you go.'

I promised I would, around ten. I said goodbye to Marina, as always, with a kiss.

'See you tomorrow,' I said.

7

But I didn't go back.

With sudden clarity, before the train had reached the second stop on my way home, I knew what I had to do. For the next two weeks, I was a whirlwind of feverish activity, putting all my affairs in order. I avoided answering the phone and managed to change my address as well as my job. As the crime stories say, I no longer frequented the usual places. In time, I was able to settle permanently in the province of La Pampa. The city of Santa Rosa enjoys a very dry climate and is located as far from the Atlantic Ocean as it is from the Pacific.

ENGINEER
SISMONDI'S
NOTEBOOK

1

My training is not in the humanities but in mathematics and physics. As an engineer, I spent in a beautiful sister country in South America only the time necessary to complete the professional job I was hired to do, little more than two months.

Having finished my task, I found myself with enough time on my hands and plenty of US dollars in my pocket. Then, taking advantage of the geographical proximity, I decided to visit the República Autónoma, that political curiosity popular magazines sometimes mention and lavishly illustrate.

I will remind the reader that this is a miniscule region located between rivers at the point where the borders of three countries meet, which confers it a certain similarity to a spider's web on the maps. There are different theories about its historical origins and ethnical composition but I shall not dwell on them in here. Its official and only language is Spanish; its currency, the US dollar.

The República Autónoma, I knew this from those magazine-pictures, amounts to an anthology of extravagancies and anachronisms. Like a medieval town, it is surrounded by a yellow battlement wall about twelve metres high. The outline of this wall is in the shape of a regular hexagon with a watchtower with narrow Gothic windows in each of its angles. On top of the walls, a path of grey stones is continuously traversed by picturesque guards poorly disguised as 14th or 15th century warriors with their shields, harquebuses and swords.

I have always felt rather dismissive of the artifices of carnival or of the stage and even more so when they are subordinated to a crass mercantile interest. I said to myself, 'The República Autónoma may just be a ridiculous show designed to fleece North American or Japanese tourists,' and urged myself not to let anyone fool me in that place, which I had already judged uncongenial but had nevertheless decided to visit.

The República Autónoma is like a small town or a big house. The vehicles arrive in it through a huge iron gate with a tiny door that almost forces you to crawl when entering it. This was the door shown to me by two colourful guards with undoubtedly European faces from the props department.

One of them led me to a small side building whose glass doors, bearing the sign ADMISSIONS OFFICE, opened up after I stepped on a rubber rectangular rug. I then found myself inside a clean modern air-conditioned office with a profusion of glass, steel and acrylics. In the middle of the strong aseptic plastic fragrance, I missed perceiving the smell of some wood, some leather. Feeling both tired and comfortable, I threw my body on a heavy chair of a somewhat perverse shape. I must have been there two or three minutes, letting my eyes wander around.

No male employees were to be seen in that office, only women going about with precise steps. They all resembled each other and they all were, within their icy style, beautiful inside their impeccable and not at all manly uniforms. Suddenly, I felt very much at ease.

Such was the path of my thoughts until a feminine voice, correct and in airline steward style with marked affectation, said through a clear microphone:

'Mr. engineer Miguel Ángel Francisco Sismondi, please go to office number 5.'

I stood up, irritated and confused by such, mocking? pomposity of calling me 'Mr. engineer.' On the other hand, I never use the name Francisco, not because I dislike it as such but because Miguel Ángel is a unit in itself and Francisco results in an unjustifiable addition. At least, that is how I've always felt about it.

Nevertheless, what importance could such detail have? Sometimes, you tend to think about what is accessory and to ignore what is fundamental, which in this case was: how did they in that office know my profession, my three names and my family name?

Office number 5, as all the others, consisted of four acrylic and Formica partitions about two metres high and it did not have its own roof. Such offices were only subdivisions of the main office. This kind of precariousness made me feel more valuable, so I sat with a deliberate negligence across from the only desk that could fit in there.

However, this mood lasted only a moment. Immediately, the general attitude of the employee taking care of me made me feel a little tense. Her impassive smile and her artificially modulated voice were this: orthopaedic devices used as means to some end. Before this professional hypocrisy, I felt, as a person with his own characteristics, totally non-existent

The woman must have been around thirty years old; I was twenty seven. In a different situation, I might perhaps have tried to establish not a relationship but some sort of communication, following that spontaneous impulse that leads us all to exchange some useless words with unknown persons. Nevertheless, such a thing was not possible with this woman. She appeared very beautiful to me with her fine features, 'chiselled,' blond hair, white and smooth skin, blue eyes..., but she seemed to me distasteful and void of any charm. Who can feel attracted to a statue or a doll?

Out of sheer discomfort and simply to do something,

I put my hand in an inner pocket of my coat to search for my documents. With her irritating put-on smile, she said, 'No document will be necessary, in the República Autónoma we believe in man's unrestricted freedom and responsibility.'

Somehow, I perceived those phrases as a skewed insult against my country where documents were certainly necessary. Soon, the blonde appeared to me more unpleasant. That's why I was happy to discover a crude sample of her intellectual want. What cause-effect relationship could there be between the two previous propositions? I was snugly enjoying this idea when the woman startled me with another inadmissible syllogism:

'Since you are Argentinean and twenty seven years old, the entrance fee in the República Autónoma is one hundred and nine US dollars.'

She drummed her malicious fingers on the PC keyboard, whose screen I could not see, and she gave me a receipt and a dollar change. She had anticipated that I would be paying her with one hundred and ten dollars. No doubt, that blonde artefact was unsettling me. As a small revenge, I thought it was worth it to ask her an ironical question, using a derisive vocative, 'Tell me, missy, what would my fee have been if I, instead of an Argentinean twenty seven year old male had been, say, an Egyptian seventy two year old lady?'

Without either reducing or increasing the magnitude of her smile and with the same flight steward's or clown's voice, she replied:

'Since that is not your case and the answer would not be of any use to you, I am not authorised to give you such irrelevant information.'

'Fuck you!' I thought and asked:

'Are we done then?'

'All set, sir. You now may go anywhere you wish. The fee gives you the right to stay for three months in the República Autónoma.'

Not because I was interested, only to be a bit annoying, I enquired:

'And with another one hundred and nine dollars will I be able to renew my stay?'

'Not at all, sir. After the three months, you must definitely leave the Republic and you can only visit it again any Tuesday in June of any year ending in 6 .'

I could have said a few more things but I chose to keep quiet.

'Take this booklet. It is free,' she added, offensively. 'It has the map of the República Autónoma, a full and detailed list of hotels, restaurants, shops, etcetera and much more information of interest.'

2

Once on the street, I leaned against a wall and began to study the map. As I've already said, the whole of the República Autónoma is nothing more than a town or, more accurately, a village or a hamlet. Its design is as simple as it is artificial, a village coldly designed on paper by architects, not a vital and distorted village naturally developed after geographical and historical whims.

It has five streets and six avenues, which are defined respectively only by their narrowness and their relative width. The five streets form other corresponding hexagons, which are proportional to the outer hexagon along which the wall runs. They are marked with the letters E, D, C, B and A. The six radial avenues, numbered 1 to 6, intersect these streets and change their number (or name), always adding up to 7 where they meet in the centre of the hexagon. I once read in the American magazine Esquire that in the centre there was a hexagonal prism about twelve metres high—the magazine gave the measurements in feet, it was made of white marble, it lacked any pictures or inscriptions and it was considered a funerary monument. It is the only monument in the Republic. This prism continued like rootstocks in underground crypts with thousands of tombs that ran along many kilometres around and beyond the borders of the República Autónoma. This was the information on Esquire but actually, when I later visited the centre of the hexagon, I couldn't find such a monument or many people who remembered its supposed previous existence.

The map of the Republic was more or less as I have drawn it here:

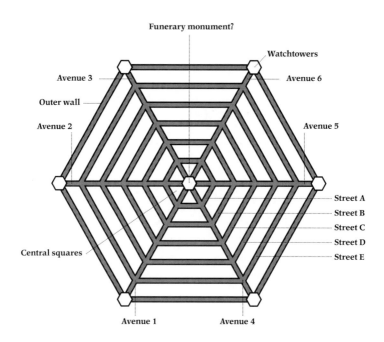

I estimated that each side of the hexagon could measure about fifteen hundred metres; I then obtained the approximate length of the apothem and, with these figures, I found that the area of the entire República Autónoma must be a little less than 6 kilometres square. As can be seen from the map, the town is subdivided into 36 blocks of buildings, 30 of them are isosceles trapezes and six are isosceles triangles, the latter taken by as many squares.

'Well' I thought, 'there is no risk of getting lost. Now to find a hotel and get a bath.'

The hotels, according to the list in the booklet, were twelve. At the rate of two per block, they were all on the A Street. I found my way along Avenue 1; I crossed streets E, D, C, and B, and arrived at A Street. Then, I walked along this hexagon, the smallest of the six, along its whole length as I progressed from the outside in.

The twelve hotels were located on the outer sidewalk of the A Street and, therefore, they all look on the central squares of the town. All had a ground floor and six stories, all looked to me identical in their design although with significant ornamental touches. However, their rates varied a great deal as I noticed when visiting the lobbies of all twelve, one by one. I don't know why there was this scattering of prices but even the most expensive of these hotels compared, for example, to the Mar del Plata rates, seemed rather cheap to me.

So, just in case, and with fresh money in my pocket, I coarsely chose the most expensive one on the A street between 1 and 4 avenues. Its name, by the way, was unconceivable for a hotel: it was Bombos y Platillos (Hype and Fanfare). Next to it was another one with a more sensible name, Excelsior. Nevertheless, in the following block was Las Dos Ardillitas, (The Two Squirrels).

An attendant, looking like a Chinese or Korean army officer, picked up my only bag and accompanied me in the lift to the fifth floor. It was a mistake on my part to offer him a tip. He rejected it angrily and stared at me as if with homicidal intentions, something that intimidated me a little. Then, he expressed his annoyance by slamming the door; I had never seen such insolence in a simple bell boy.

I decided not to give any more thought to the Chinese man. The room was excellent. 'I have chosen well,' I thought. 'No doubt, other hotels must be hiding their deficiencies.'

The bathroom was impeccable. Feeling happy all of a sudden, I gave myself to the delights of the shower, the hot water, the aromatic soap and the fluffy towels.

While I was lazily dressing, a sensation of weariness and tiredness, usual after a long trip, was invading me. It was nine pm. I could have gone to bed immediately but I know that going to bed without dinner will mean waking up many times afterwards.

'The best thing to do will be to go out and eat something, and then tomorrow I can take a walk around the town.'

I then heard a distant thunder and could see through the window, against a very dark sky, the zigzag of far away lightning. In view of that, I took my umbrella and went down on the lift.

I walked along avenue 4 and turned left on D Street. From what little I saw in those four or five blocks, I inferred that, whether I wanted it or not, the town had plenty of charm. The houses were the materialisation of medieval or Renaissance prints except that they were favoured by electricity, by gas, by running water. The street lighting, provided by iron lamps of singular forms, was perfect. Roads and pavements were extremely clean, and I could not help recalling the dirtiness of the streets of Buenos Aires and the disregard of its inhabitants, so rigorously scrupulous concerning their bodies and their houses.

There was hardly any traffic, and the reason was clear. Why drive vehicles in such a small town? I could see beautiful vintage cars rolling by like those I sometimes watched as a child in Argentinean streets. But these cars appeared brand new or at least restored to the last detail and repainted with lively colours. I saw a deep red '37 Hudson Terraplane, a '46 Renault, long and flat and yellow, an enormous white '42 Lincoln... What gorgeous automobiles!

I then realised that I was beginning to like everything I saw and congratulated myself for visiting the República Autónoma. In contrast, the unpleasant memory of the agent in the Admissions Office came back to me. What nationality could she be? She pronounced the Spanish more or less like the Argentineans and the Uruguayans but she buzzed some violent 's' that we would have frowned on in Rio de la Plata. Her somewhat pale figure made me infer that she could be German or Austrian but then I thought she must rather be an Italian from Milan or Turin...'The hell with it!' I scolded myself for thinking about that disagreeable woman. 'What do I care about her?'

On the corner of D Street and Avenue 6, there was an attractive restaurant with decorated wooden panels on its walls in a sort of imitation of an Alpine landscape. I expected to see a German name but, incredibly, it was called El Rincón del Pelado Juancito (Johnny the Bald).

I sat at a table next to a wall and started to ravenously read the menu. Actually, I do not know why I do this since I invariably end up choosing one of the simplest dishes. On that occasion, I ordered as often before, a chicken escalope with chips, a dish that never disappoints me. The names of the wines were completely unknown to me so I made a random selection and ordered a Burgundy called Podestà. I read the label carefully but could not find out its country of origin. To allay my curiosity, I said to the waiter:

'What a good wine! What country does it come from?'

'I don't know, sir,' he replied with an irritated insolence. 'How would I know?'

'I bet he is a relative of the lady in the Admissions Office,' I thought and decided not to address him again.

In the same row as mine, opposite me, three tables away, I saw a woman that was on her own, around twenty five years old. My attention was immediately held. Indeed, she was not a woman to go unobserved. She would have been at least 1.75 metres high. She had a good figure, slim but curvaceous with splendid dark curly hair that shook as she moved her head.

From her clothes, her manners, her gestures and the way she moved her lips as well as her panache, I judged her Argentinean. I was entranced by her hair, which awakened in me a desire to put my fingers in it and caress it from the nape of the neck to the top. I also discovered that she had large dark eyes and deep black long eyebrows... Her contrived nose was the typical result of plastic surgery; no doubt, a curved and bigger and prettier nose had previously occupied that spot. 'A Semitic nose' I thought. 'This must be an Argentinean of Sephardic or Arab ascendants.' It is part of my second nature, the constant habit of guessing a person's stock guided by their countenance.

For a very brief moment, her eyes met mine. It was less than a second but that was enough to tingle me with yearning and restlessness. I set myself a duty both pleasant and unpleasant, how to start a conversation with her. The circumstances were favourable: we were both without company, we were compatriots and we were the same age... I had to find a way to... Suddenly, I realised that for no reason I was feeling nervous and my legs were shaking. How, in an instant, could I have switched from my more or less usual poise to a state of extreme idiocy?

'What would happen,' I thought, 'if I approach her table and say something to her?' I tried to reason and see what results I could expect at each end of this action. The best odds were that she would accept my approach, that she answered something and that we initiated some kind of dialogue. However, it could also be that she stayed silent or rejected me coldly or even harshly. At any rate, she would make a fool of me, which is what I most fear in the world. A muddle of sterile ideas came then to my mind, while timidity and indecision made me feel paralysed. Looking for a sort of mental shake-up, I turned my eyes away.

Seconds later, it wasn't the dark eyes that were in front of me but a man's back. No doubt, she had been waiting for him, as could be inferred from the familiarity evident in their conversation. Stupidly, I felt a great sense of relief, as that man's presence freed me from the heavy responsibility of approaching the beautiful woman. They were a couple, and I could not reasonably do anything. This way, I was not guilty of being shy or irresolute.

That's what I thought but the truth was that my eyes returned continuously to the point where an accursed back had interposed itself between a pair of dark eyes and me.

The weariness of the trip and the torpor of the meal and the wine were overcoming me. Unwillingly, I smoked one last cigarette. When I paid the bill I saw that the dinner turned out to be rather cheap so I decided to eat every evening at El Rincón del Pelado Juancito, not so much out of convenience, as with the hope of seeing that Jewish or Arab woman again.

Out on the street, I found that it was pouring, so much so that you could hardly make out the houses across the road. And yet the noise of the rain had hardly been heard inside the restaurant. I congratulated myself for my wisdom in bringing my umbrella.

In front of the restaurant, there were five or six impressive carriages pulled by young and spirited stallions. Although I was only a few blocks away from the Bombos y Platillos hotel, walking would have meant getting soaked through, so I opened my umbrella, quickly crossed the road and jumped into that taxi from a bygone period. A few minutes later, tired and happy, I was in my hotel bed. I had no time to think of the impressive dark woman because sleep soon got the best of me.

3

On the third day of my stay in the República Autónoma, I was sorry to have wasted one hundred and nine dollars in order to visit it. After the initial dazzle and surprise, I was now fed up with that small town. I had already walked around it heaven knows how many times and found no reason at all to go on reiterating at that stage that, what, at the beginning, had seduced me.

On the other hand, one small worry had me annoyed, small enough but a worry all the same. I have always been a hearty eater and a lover of good and abundant food. Added to this was my delight in leisure and siestas, things forbidden to me in Buenos Aires. These were resulting in a weight increase that was starting to worry me. Not that I was remotely considering to give up such pleasures.

I was a loner and took pleasure in being one. Every now and then, I watched groups of tourists with their profusion of cameras and gathered around by their nationalities. I had made the mistake of travelling alone and now I could not find the way to enjoy a minimum of social life with somebody.

Therefore, I wandered aimlessly. I was sure the woman in the restaurant had by now left the country. I had not seen her again, either at El Rincón del Pelado Juancito or during any of my boring walks around the town. Neither had I seen again the man whose presence had frustrated my unlikely approach.

Perhaps out of my loneliness, I thought of her often but the details were nebulous. I could only remember her vaguely as an overall impression apart from the distinct exception of her black dazzling eyes and her profuse dark hair, which led me to elaborate erotic fantasies.

I had had enough with the República Autónoma. The third night, already packed, I went to bed with the decision to leave the country next day. That was the easiest thing in the world.

From the outer wall, one had to walk about one kilometre to reach the Carretera del Inti where twice daily, at 10 am and 6 pm, you could catch the bus and reach the central airport three hours later.

Because I got up a little late and was feeling lazy, I decided to miss the 10 am bus and postpone my departure until 6 pm. I don't usually take breakfast, so just to have something to do I entered a bar and sat at a table in front of the window and ordered some coffee, which really was only a pretext to light the first cigarette of the day.

Following what seems mandatory in the República Autónoma, the waiter brought me as a gift, together with the coffee, a copy of the latest number of *La Voz Autónoma*, the only newspaper printed in the town. Actually, the term newspaper is somewhat disproportionate as *La Voz Autónoma* is merely a four-page leaflet in magazine format. I had tried to read it before, and it had always been impossible. The paper is of good quality, the printing careful, the errors few. Nevertheless, I never succeeded in learning what *La Voz Autónoma* was talking about. It was as if the writers were sharing a series of tacit implications with the readers that were completely alien to me. The totality of the news was local without even a single international item of the sort that is simultaneously read in the whole world and which, by the way, mean nothing to the reader. For example, a train-crash in Belgium or a flood in Pakistan. From the first to the last line, the entire *La Voz Autónoma* carried news like this one:

SATISFACTION OF VALDEZ

It is inferred from the letter sent yesterday to Pereyra by the notary. Nevertheless, observers judge that an agreement can hardly be reached before the end of the week and, if it occurs, the agreement would not be long lasting. On the other hand, the emissaries have censored the cosmetic details, and this seems to bring nearer the solution to the problem. Let us hope that, for the benefit of Dr. Elena Stone, it will be so.

Be that as it may, I wasn't willing to waste my time decoding news that, whatever they said, did not concern me. I leaned back on my chair and, already on my second cigarette, I watched through the window the contour of a pink and greyish cloud.

Then, on the opposite pavement, I saw the longed-for-woman. Her right arm was holding the left arm of the same man I had seen previously. He was now wearing a speckled sport jacket, a shirt opened on the first button and a 'kerchief around his neck. She wore denim jeans and a pale blue pullover to show off her splendid figure.

I watched the couple attentively, positive that they did not see me. They were chatting distractedly, as if neither cared very much what the other was saying. This lack of bother, far from being an incentive to me, showed that their relationship was pretty intimate and old, as to make them leave aside certain courtesies.

In line with the Argentine style of ignoring traffic rules, they started crossing the road diagonally toward the café windows. I now gladly noticed that the man was not only shorter than me but also shorter than the woman. He was, however, handsome and elegant, smartly dressed, and his appearance denoted economic comfort.

I focused my eyes on the woman's face. More precisely, they were fixed on the black lake of her eyes. An instant before stepping on the pavement, her eyes met mine, stopping for a few seconds without her companion noticing it.

Then, when she reached my window, the woman put her left hand in her back pocket, pulled out a piece of paper and let it fall on the pavement. Anxiety and emotion made me stand up immediately and run to the street. From the bar's door, I saw the couple walking away. The paper was folded several times. I picked it up and, not daring to read it in such circumstances, I kept it in my pocket.

I reached the bar at vertiginous speed, paid for my coffee and ran to the Bombos y Platillos hotel. Not wishing to wait for the lift, I climbed the stairs to the fifth floor and reached my room, which I locked.

Before unfolding the paper, I took some seconds to dream, out of vanity, of the possibility that this might be a love message. But how could she have had it ready? How could she have foreseen a chance encounter with me? And worse still, did she even remember my existence? Had I perhaps become a perceptible being for her?

I sat on the edge of the bed, unfolded the tight rectangular paper and I read:

Meu nome é Isabel Simes e sou acusada de um delito que não cometi e que é punido com a pena de morte. Por favor, avise a meu pai, José Simes: Avenida Nossa Senhora de Copacabana, 2005, Rio de Janeiro, Brasil.

My name is Isabel Simes, and I am being accused of a crime I did not commit and that carries the death penalty. Please inform my father, José Simes:
Avenida Nossa Senhora de Copacabana, 2005, Rio de Janeiro, Brazil.

I read the message two or three more times, unsure of how to organise my thoughts. The paper was one-half of a page pulled from a Brazilian agenda with a calendar and a legend printed in Portuguese. The text was written with a blue ballpoint pen in a careful and slightly childish manner. The handwriting and its care showed me that Isabel Simes had been able to write the message calm enough but then, for a reason I could not tell, had to put the paper hurriedly in her pocket until she found the opportunity to send the message to some recipient or other. That casual recipient turned out to be me, and perhaps the sudden appearance of the man now walking with her had forced the girl to hide the paper. Therefore, I assumed, somehow that the man was an enemy of Isabel Simes. If so, why were they walking together in such a relaxed and amiable fashion?

Suddenly, I decided to change my attitude. None of that was of my concern, and yet I was beginning to make elaborated conjectures. However, I read the message again, asking for help and the words *'um delito que não cometi e que é punido com a pena de morte'* eclipsed the rest and made me feel a bit alarmed.

At the beginning, I thought of writing to José Simes but what and what for? I decided then on the simplest and more reasonable (and least compromising) resort. I copied on the back of an envelope José Simes' address and then I put the fretful message in it although unsigned. The daughter's own handwriting would be more telling than any phrase I might add. 'Besides,' I prudently thought, 'this method avoids my getting into something that doesn't concern me.'

I have always preferred taking decisions, maybe even a wrong decision, to not taking any decision at all, as the uncertainty makes me nervous and paralyses me. I had just made a choice and I calmly walked to the post office. This was a glittery office with abundant steel, glass and plastic that looked very recently built. I posted José Simes the letter by registered mail, and there ended my problem.

Once in the street, I attempted to build a mental defence wall. I did not want to think about Isabel Simes' message, I did not want to think, would not think...

As a reflex movement that has accompanied me for years, I have the habit of checking my watch without reading the time.

I repeated this tic five or six times and realised that again I was actually very nervous. As some stabilising element, I did read the time carefully. It was already 11:30 in the morning.

I suddenly felt absolutely and fearfully sick of the República Autónoma. A desperate urge to leave it took hold of me, which now seemed to me - how shall I put it? - correct and wicked.

I cursed myself for not having taken the 10 o'clock bus. I still had some six hours to kill in that abominable place. To diminish the wait, I intended to leave the República Autónoma at four o'clock in the afternoon. I preferred to wait for the six o'clock bus outdoors, in the middle of the countryside, next to the road of the Inti, sitting on my case and smoking, rather than in the wary comfort of my room in the hotel Bombos y Platillos.

Everything about those streets, fit for a cheap musical, felt unpleasant to me, beginning with the hypocritical faces of their inhabitants. Back in the hotel, when I asked for the key to my room, the caretaker gave me an envelope, saying, 'They left this for you.'

It was a large envelope of the type called Legal, all white and with a single typed word: sismondi. I opened it impatiently while travelling in the lift. I extracted a small unfolded piece of paper. The top had a letterhead with the coat of arms of the República Autónoma. One centimetre below, a typed note—written on an old and faulty machine that rose the a's and lowered the o's.

The text read, *'Por favor presentese obligatoriamente en la Oficina 17 del Poder Judicial a la una de la tarde.'*

'Please report by order at Office 17 of the Judicial Power at one o'clock.'

I entered my room. I calmly closed the door, locked it, sat in front of the table, lit a cigarette and re-examined the official document. The typewriter used, of an ordinary cursive font, was not only defective but also quite dirty as shown by the grey smudged contours of the letters. They had first written 'fabor' and then hammered twice or thrice the v over the b without taking the care to apply some correcting fluid or at least an eraser. The necessary accent on the second e from the word 'presentese' had been omitted. Besides, the text, occupying a line and a half, was almost stuck to the letterhead, so the lower section of the sheet, 90% of it, was blank.

These various flaws told me that whoever wrote the summons was a very clumsy person with little learning.

'Please report by order at Office 17 of the Judicial Power at one o'clock.' No more, no less. No date, no addressee, no title, no greeting, no signature...not even a punctuation mark that would for an instant interrupt such a drawn out worm of black characters.

I had already lit another cigarette that I consumed voraciously, almost without stopping, to the point that I felt a little sick like a beginner. I put the butt-end in the ashtray and, urged by I don't know what idea, ran to the bathroom and threw away the acknowledgment of the letter I had sent to José Simes. I then flushed the toilet several times.

That act helped me to recover my composure, and I thought of getting suitably ready for what might happen to me...What might happen to me? Was I mad? What could happen to me? Bah, bah, bah! Nonsense...!

And yet I was getting all my personal documents ready. ('No document will be necessary, in the República Autónoma we believe in man's unrestricted freedom and responsibility.') I had punctiliously counted my money in the currency of three countries and piled up the notes in three groups from the largest to the smallest and on the same face, as bank tellers do. Then, I carefully put everything in the briefcase.

With the pretext of the cold, I had put on a matching high school graduate ensemble of grey trousers and blue coat, a pale blue shirt. A blue and red tie from my football club and a grey pullover completed my gear. I looked at myself in the mirror, straightened the collar of my shirt and adjusted my tie. I feel safer when I am smartly dressed.

Just in case, I kept my glasses in an inside pocket of my jacket although I only need them when reading a very long time. Likewise, I took the three ballpoint pens—two blue ones and a red one—which, as an obsessive person, I have always carried with me wherever I went. I also added this ninety-six page hard-back notebook of the Rivadavia brand in which I usually put diverse observations or impressions. (In my Buenos Aires home, I keep a great deal of these notebooks, all full from beginning to end. Really, I don't know what function they can perform but there they are. Sometimes, I have tried to use them for writing short stories, sometimes poems, but reading them again I realised that they weren't much good.) But in the present case, this Rivadavia notebook has allowed me to set down all that had happened since my arrival in the República Autónoma up to this very moment.

Before going down, I grabbed the whisky bottle I habitually take with me in all my trips and drank a sizeable gulp. Now more invigorated, I walked to Office 17 of the Judicial Power. I had seen it many times, it was on Avenue 1 between A and B streets but, frankly, I don't believe Offices 16 or 18, or any other, existed.

4

The justice officer was a mannered person with a sickly gaze. He wore a pair of tight bottle green trousers and a shiny white shirt with fine green vertical strips. Instead of a tie, he exhibited, that is the word, a ridiculous and enormous green bow that matched his tight trousers, striped shirt and sickly eyes.

A desk with a thick glass top separated us. Under it, there were postcards with seascapes, some paper flowers, a sticker with the words DO NOT SMOKE, FOR EVERYBODY´S BENEFIT and another, LET US TREAT EACH OTHER SWEETLY. There was also an aged picture of an actor from the silent cinema that I couldn't quite recognize and a couple of cuttings from a sports magazine with photographs of the famous football player, Pelé, with the white Santos shirt in one and with the yellow Brazilian selection in another.

The justice officer noticed my look because he asked me:

'Do you like football?'

I wanted to avoid all needless conversation, so instead of answering the truth I said:

'Not much.'

'But you showed interest in those pictures.'

'Well, I recognised Pelé...everybody knows him.'

I didn't want to add anything more, and the arrival of an orderly bringing coffee saved me from having to continue talking.

'Sugar or saccharin?' the officer asked me.

'Sugar,' I replied, somewhat mechanically. I had just seen that the orderly was the same Chinese or Korean man that worked as a bellboy in the Bombos y Platillos hotel.

'Me, too, I used to take my coffee with sugar until two or three months ago,' the justice officer said, not noticing that my eyes were following the orderly. 'My mother, instead, always drank her coffee with saccharin. One day... Are you listening to me?'

'Yes, of course,' I turned toward him.

'As I was telling you, one day I am at home, I want to drink some coffee...but can't find the sugar anywhere. I ask my mother, 'Mammy, and the sugar...?' She says, 'Oh, Marcelo, we are out of it, I forgot to get some. Just for now, how about some saccharin?' Done, that day I took my coffee with saccharine and... well..., I got so used to it that I no longer could drink it with sugar.'

He smiled and fixed his eyes on me, as if waiting for an answer. What did I care about that story of sugar and saccharin? Then I gave him a stupid answer:

'Well, yes...They say man is a creature of habits.'

Apparently disappointed, the justice officer adopted a maternal attitude.

'But...! Why are you so jumpy...? I have tried to have a conversation with you about trivial subjects to make you relax a little, so you would feel comfortable and could defend yourself better. But I can see I have failed. Would you prefer it if we went right to the crux of the matter?'

'That's right. I want to end this nuisance as soon as possible as I shall be leaving the República Autónoma in three hours time and I still have my packing to do.'

'A lie is a bad start which won't benefit you in the future,' the officer replied.

'What do you mean by that?' I said, angry and defiant.

The officer smiled in a loathsome manner, accusing me with his index finger in a way that for him sought to be funny.

'Your nose is going to grow like Pinocchio's. Why do you say you still have your case to pack if you had everything ready last night?'

'What do you know?' I said, inferring that the easily influenced Chinese must have been the informant.

The officer abandoned his playful tone and suddenly became serious.

'Well, the cases are not the main thing in this problem. You'll want to know why you have been summoned, right?'

I nodded, beginning to feel lethargic. The air was a little stale, and I was now starting to see the officer as very far away or as a bad memory.

'Right,' he added, looking at me steadily, 'I'll tell you, then. I beg you to take it calmly.'

He waited a few seconds, intending to intimidate me.

Then, with a softer voice, as if it were a secret between us, he whispered, 'there are two serious charges against you.'

'Bah!' I replied, suddenly not just unconcerned but about to burst with laughter, that crude dramatising by the officer had liberated me from any fear. 'It must be some mistake.'

Then with an incredibly effeminate tone, effeminate as extreme as the coarsest theatrical parody, the justice officer exclaimed:

'What a man this is! What a hard-headed man!' and he knocked on the glass of the desk with his knuckles, as if weighing in his mind my lack of brains. 'My dear friend,' he continued, placing his hand on mine, which I withdrew violently, 'I have tried to help you,' he suddenly lost all amiability, 'going beyond my duty, and I only get mockery and contempt from you. Therefore, I will limit myself to read the two serious charges and make no comment at all.'

'That's exactly what I want.'

'Very well. Let's see where the devil,' he returned to his playful mannered style, 'is your naughty file. Let's see, let's see, let's see...'

Humming in bolero rhythm, he poked around for a while inside the drawers of his desk and pulled out a black folder, old and dusty, that obviously had not been used for many years.

'First charge,' he declaimed, pretending to read from the folder, which he was displaying as a screen between him and me, 'you are charged with destroying the ecological balance, in the degree of attempt with likely eventual success.'

He paused and glanced at me from over the folder with ridiculous seriousness. I answered with a disproportionate smile and an unconcerned movement of my arm, urging him to continue.

'Second charge, you are charged with perverting the course of justice in the degree of attempt.'

'Ah,' I pretended to be interested in that stupid nonsense, 'I understand that I am being accused of attempting to commit crimes, not actually of committing crimes, is that right?'

'That is correct, sir. No one can commit crimes in the República Autónoma. Justice that sees it all always makes the crime aborted before it is committed. But it is our duty nevertheless to punish even the attempt.'

While pronouncing his last phrases and, with his index finger wet with spit, he tried to curl his eyelashes. I felt omnipotent.

'Very well. I tell you that you cannot deceive me. That dirty folder has not been used in many years, and you have only pretended to read something that is nowhere written. May I?' And I grabbed the folder abruptly.

I opened it randomly and then went through its pages. Printed with PC dots, all pages from top to bottom repeated with total accuracy my three given names and my surname, my ID number, my addresses in Buenos Aires and, in the República Autónoma, my date of arrival in the country, my... They also repeated these words: First charge, you are charged with destroying the ecological balance...

'But...,' I muttered, astonished, 'do you mean that all pages in this folder say exactly the same thing?'

The officer rested his elbows on the desk and his face between the palms of his hands. Watching me with a dreamful pose, he specified:

'Not only all of this folder's pages but all the pages of all the folders in this office say the same thing. When someone attempts to commit a crime justice publishes it numerous times so no one will forget it.'

5

The black marble stairs had fifteen steps with two dark iron banisters and it ended blindly against the wall. They had a landing of about two metres square with a high and hard chair on it in the style of a monastery or a church. A judge was sitting on the chair. Furthermore, this judge was dressed more or less like an 18th century gentleman as I remembered from schoolbooks pictures. He even wore a white curled wig.

I had been placed at the bottom of the stairs, sitting in front of a small Formica table on which, who knows why, there was a cheap paper block, a black pencil and a rubber eraser. Those stairs leading nowhere were rather steep, and in order to see the judge I was forced to take a quite uncomfortable posture with my head leaning backwards to an extreme.

'My friend Sismondi,' the judge said. His voice sounded inexpressive and tired with some resignation or wisdom. 'I am a simple and honest man. I dislike sitting on top of these extravagant stairs in these ridiculous clothes or putting on this wig smelling of naphthalene. I am only doing it out of respect for the traditions of the República Autónoma... But, between us, I would like to see these anachronisms disappear one day. A couple of months ago, I submitted as an ordinary citizen a modernisation project. In it, I propose, among other advantages, to eliminate many of these elements, which without intending to offend anyone, we could call histrionic.'

Histrionic elements, the judge had just found the right term that I wanted to describe all those ceremonies and stage sets, and I could not but entirely agree with him.

The judge produced the red packet of Jockey Club cigarettes. He took out one, lit it and let out a heavy puff of smoke. I had never seen an 18th century man smoking Argentinean cigarettes. The judge took my attentive look as a tacit request and threw me a cigarette and a matchbox. Although I had a packet of rough local cigarettes called El Gran Automóvil, I wanted to taste the familiar Jockey again. I lit it, and the judge indicated with a gesture that I could keep the matches.

'Well,' I thought, 'all will be easier with this straightforward and reasonable man.'

After some further puffs, the judge, with the look of someone who wants to put a small but annoying problem out of the way and move on to more important things, said:

'Right then, Sismondi, the thing is this. You can see that there is no prosecutor here nor any defence counsellor nor jury, no ushers, no secretaries, no policemen and no public either. All these people are more of an encumbrance than of help. Only you and I are here, luckily. Both of us will be able to reach an agreement and do justice without so much awkward red tape. Do you agree?'

'Excellent!' I exclaimed, feeling some thrill. 'I have been talking to the justice officer and I didn't find him a reasonable man.'

'Who did you talk to? Pérez, López, Gómez, Juárez or Suárez?'

'I don't know, he never told me his name. He is a little mannered....'

(I instantly remembered that the officer's name was Marcelo but I didn't feel like telling the judge).

'All five officers are mannered,' the judge corroborated. 'It happens that they usually feel sorry for the accused and they then try to sweeten their manners.'

'Well,' I interrupted, as the subject did not interest me. 'But, whoever he was, I didn't find him a reasonable man.' For me, it was important to establish this adverse conclusion.

'Nevertheless, he is a reasonable man in his own way. Only fools think there is a single logic in this world. Right?'

'True,' I admitted. What the judge had just said appeared both notorious and irrefutable.

'All right,' the judge said, applauding. 'The matter is very plain, and we can solve it in ten minutes if you agree with me. You already know the two charges against you...Only that you must admit your guilt, put your little signature here... end of story.'

'Admit my guilt? But I don't feel guilty of anything...'

'You are forcing me to enter into subjectivities here.' The judge seemed to wither, as with a tiredness of years. 'And on this issue it will be hard to agree, I beg you to put aside whatever you feel or don't feel and declare yourself openly and plainly guilty. This will facilitate things, you see?' and he emphasised his words with a knowing smile and wink.

I smiled, too. I had realised that if I admitted the charges, the judge would acquit me after 'having cooperated with justice' or something similar.

'I think I understand,' I cautiously assented. 'Assuming I declare myself guilty...Then, when can I leave the República Autónoma?'

'Never,' the judge replied, shrugging his shoulders and opening his hands as if to show that he felt obliged to give an obvious answer to a not very bright pupil.

'Never?' I repeated with some stammering. 'What do you mean, never?'

'All crimes carry a death sentence. You will be hanged and then buried in the pantheon of foreign criminals in our underground cemetery. And it is not allowed to exhume or relocate bodies. Therefore, you will never be able to leave the República dead or alive.'

'But, your Honour, are you mocking me? Before, didn't you say that we both could reach an agreement in ten minutes?'

'And where is the contradiction, if I may know? The agreement, as I told you, is that you accept your guilt. That way, it will all be very simple and without any red tape. You admit to your guilt, you are hanged immediately, you are buried and that's the end of the story.' He rubbed his hands to give a sense of efficiency.

'No, sir,' I said with energy, 'no way. I cannot accept this absurd approach. All you want is not having to work...'

'No one likes doing needless work. And I am already

ninety-two years old and feeling rather tired...'

'...I am not going to let myself be killed just so you can have less work.' I thought the judge must have been seventy at the most, never the ninety-two he had proclaimed.

'I think you are a little selfish.' The judge shook his head disapprovingly. 'And you are delegating the problem. It is not a question of whether or not I want to work. I am a public servant and I am devoted to my community as it should be... But, after all, you are within your rights not to admit your guilt. In such case, I will be obliged to make you understand, rationally, of course, that you have committed a crime. The question is, are you ready to have a rational conversation with me, free of emotionalisms and exaltations with the only purpose of finding the truth?'

'Of course.'

'Very well. Do you recognise this writing?' He produced the now open envelope of the letter I had posted to José Simes.

'Naturally,' I answered, far from being intimidated, 'it's my own writing, and that is the letter I sent to Brazil. And you, your Honour, will realise you have committed a crime by interfering, opening and reading my correspondence.'

'Are you familiar with our laws?'

'I have no need to be familiar with them. I imagine that interfering with correspondence has to be a crime anywhere in the world.'

'You imagine, imagine...' He drew some spirals in the air. 'To imagine is an easy thing...But you don't know for sure, you are talking without knowing the facts, you talk because air is free. They are all like that.'

I felt on my face and ears a heated wave of homicidal fervour against that accursed old man.

'At any rate,' he continued, 'even assuming I committed a crime, it's not you who should or could judge me. Remember that the issue is a different one. I am trying to prove that you attempted to pervert the course of justice. This is the flagrant evidence, you posted a letter to the father of a woman who is condemned by the law. What did you do it for?'

'She asked me to.'

'I asked you about the purpose, not the cause. I know that you did it because she asked you to.' He pointed Isabel Simes's paper toward me. 'But I need to know what you did it for.'

'In her message, Isabel Simes says she has been convicted of a crime she didn't commit...'

'Of course, very well,' he emphasised with irony, 'and you immediately believe Isabel Simes, absolutely dismissing what our justice has established. Evidently, Isabel Simes is very pretty and that no doubt influenced you, so you wanted to help her. We, naturally, have stopped that letter from leaving our borders and reaching Brazil. What would have happened if we hadn't taken such wise precaution? Do you know?'

'I don't know and I don't care.'

'I will tell you. Said José Simes would have shown up here, he would have demanded reports, attempted to recover his daughter alive and ended by referring to the Brazilian government, which in turn would have filed diplomatic complaints and perhaps made threats of invasion and war... etcetera. Look at the international problem that your alarmist attitude could have created. Our country, as you can see, is very small and weak, and precisely for that reason we must act with much prudence.'

At this point, I was no longer interested in defending myself but instead wanted to show the judge my contempt and hate.

'I'll have you know that I would be the first one to rejoice if the Brazilian Army and Air Force annihilate this cursed República Autónoma.'

'You will not wound my patriotism,' the judge answered coldly. 'The question is, if your letter had reached Brazil, could that have created some problem?'

'I believe and wish that it would be so,' I replied arrogantly.

'You believe or you are sure?'

'I am sure,' I said proudly and at the same time with frustration for not having managed to originate that gratifying problem.

'In other words,' the judge concluded, 'you tried to subvert the course of justice. Yes or no?'

'Yes but that is a pseudo justice, a ridiculous kind of justice.'

'I am not interested in your opinions. I am only concerned that you have said yes. That means you have admitted to the second charge, which reads like this, 'You are charged with perverting the course of justice in the degree of attempt.'

He descended the stairs and placed a paper on my table.

'Sign here,' he said, handing me a beautiful fountain pen.

I quickly read that I admitted having attempted to subvert, etcetera.

'I will sign nothing,' I declared and I crossed my arms.

'Very well,' said the judge, as if distressed by a hostile attitude he didn't deserve. Then, ostentatiously, and in very large characters so I could read it, he wrote: The prisoner admits his crime and, his fingers being stiff due to his rheumatism, he cannot sign and he authorises me, the Judge, to place it on record, considering the acted present as sufficient and definite proof, no allegation to the contrary being admissible. An unintelligible signature followed and under it, a stamp with the words 'the acting judge'.

I burst out laughing.

'What is this clowning about? Don't make me laugh! What kind of justice is this? Are you really a judge? You are a poor imbecile!'

I don't remember exactly everything I said. I know I insulted him as much as I could, not sparing coarse or four-letter words so I could humiliate that idiot disguised as a Versailles courtier.

After this joyful angered explosion, I kept the most absolute silence, no longer wanting to discuss or object to anything as that amounted to be a part of his game and give it some kind of validity.

Distractedly, I heard how the judge was proving that I had attempted 'to destroy the ecological balance with likely eventual success.' It was something like many animals possess, a kind of defence in their own intimidating size. So the elephant is an animal no other can even dream of attacking. Other, much smaller animals simulate a good deal larger size in the face of danger, as many birds do when they inflate their feathering. These changes momentarily confuse their potential enemies and may even induce a fleeting anguish in them. However, this cannot be justified when the victim is a person or a peaceful animal like the noble, useful and hard-working horse. I had to remember that during my first night in the República Autónoma, besieged by the rain, I had opened my umbrella in front of the horse that pulled the carriage that would return me to the Bombos y Platillos hotel. No doubt, the horse took me for a dangerous animal, increasing its size before attacking and perhaps killing him. That horse's distress, although ephemeral, might reduce its life for some minute or hours, something that would unfailingly provoke some unbalance in the ecological system.

Before such outlandish perversities, I continued keeping a dignified silence. I did not even unfold my arms or glance when the judge again ostentatiously wrote that I admitted the terms of this charge and that suffering from rheumatism, etcetera, etcetera.

He climbed the stairs once again, sat behind his desk and now shouting with a voice already ninety-two years old and breaking with the frogs of senility and, as if he wished to be heard by a crowd, dictated that I would be hanged on an unspecified date but exactly ten minutes after the hanging of the 'conspiring Brazilian who, out of decorum, shall herein remain nameless.'

6

For five days, I have been living in the small apartment that justice has assigned me and which they say is my provisional prison. I have all the things necessary to live comfortably. Since I also have all the time I may want, I have devoted and continue to devote myself to writing this report on the Rivadavia notebook I have previously mentioned.

The living room is very pleasant with a small coffee table and semicircular armchairs. On the table, there are fine-looking ashtrays, cigarettes, glasses, a container full of ice cubes and a variety of drinks. I must admit that justice has provided me with all I have asked for. Since it is my belief that even in the worst situations we can find positive things, rather than give myself to laments and despair I am drinking whisky on the rocks and smoking. Since I like whisky and I like smoking, what else, apart from sheer stoicism, would it be to give them up now?

Some three minutes ago, the telephone rang, and I had to pick it up. This was the first time I heard Isabel Simes' supposed voice. Her sobbing, her anguish, the Portuguese language made it difficult to understand her immediately. Nevertheless, I understood at least three things: Isabel was reproaching me for not having warned José Simes, Isabel informed me that she was on the way to be hanged, Isabel was calling me a *covarde*. Imagining her dark hair and the black lake of her eyes, I couldn't or wouldn't explain to her that her accusation was unfair. I would let my frustrated love die despising him who had not known how to defend her.

I was more concerned with checking the time and, from that moment, started counting the ten minutes the judge had dictated. At the same time, I kissed the silver cross I always wear around my neck and I prayed a Lord's Prayer and a Hail Mary, a Lord's Prayer and a Hail Mary, a Lord's Prayer and a Hail Mary...

When the ninth minute arrived I served myself another whisky and drank it in one flash. I immediately heard some steps that stopped at my door. Before they introduced the key in the lock, I seemed to hear some persons trying to hold back their giggles.

I really don't know yet whether these people are acting seriously or playing a joke on me. If God grants me a tomorrow, I shall try to establish it.

PICCIRILLI

For some time now, my bookshelves have been filled to capacity. I should have them enlarged but the wood and the labour are costly, and I prefer to postpone those expenses and favour other more urgent needs. I adopted the temporary solution of placing the books horizontally and so managed to make better use of the available space.

We know that books, whether placed vertically or horizontally, gather dust, bugs and spider webs. I have neither the patience nor the inclination to do the regular cleaning that would be necessary.

Several months ago on a foggy Saturday, I finally decided to take out one by one all the books and brush them and rub the shelves with a damp cloth.

On one of the lower shelves, I found Piccirilli. In spite of the dust to be seen in those corners, his aspect was, as usual, impeccable. But that, I noticed only later. At first, he looked to me like a bit of cord or a portion of cloth but I was wrong, it was from head to foot Piccirilli. That is, it was a tiny but proper man five centimetres tall.

Absurdly, it seemed odd to me that he should be dressed. There certainly was no reason for him to be naked, and the fact that Piccirilli is so small does not authorise us to think of him as an animal. To be more accurate, I was not so much surprised because he was dressed but by how he was dressed. He wore high wide-mouthed boots, an ample flapped jacket and a gauzy shirt with lace edging and he carried a feather on his hat and a sword on his waist.

With his spiky moustache and his pointed beard,

Piccirilli was the living reduced facsimile of D'Artagnan, the hero of *The Three Musketeers*, as I remembered him from old illustrations.

Now, why did I name him Piccirilli and not D'Artagnan as would seem logical? I think that, especially, for two complementary reasons. The first one is that his sharp pointed physique literally demands the small i's in Piccirilli and, therefore, rejects the more robust a's in D'Artagnan. The second reason is that when I talked to him in French he didn't understand a word, which showed me that since he was no Frenchman, neither could he be D'Artagnan.

Piccirilli must be around fifty years old as some white strands run through his dark hair. That is how I estimate his age, the same as with beings of our size. But I don't really know if time prescribes identical proportions to beings as tiny as Piccirilli. Seeing him so minute, one tends, perhaps unjustifiably, to think that his life is shorter and that his time runs faster than ours, as we learn by looking at bugs and insects.

Who can tell? And even if such is the case, how then can we explain that Piccirilli is wearing 17th century attire? Can we accept that Piccirilli is nearly four hundred years old? Piccirilli, that creature that hardly occupies any space at all, can he really be entitled to so much time? Piccirilli, a being with such a flimsy appearance?

I should like to pose these and other questions to Piccirilli and that he would answer. I often do question him, and Piccirilli does answer me but he doesn't manage to make himself understood, and I don't even know if he understands my questions. He listens to me, yes, and he looks attentive and then, as soon as I stop, he quickly answers. But in what language does Piccirilli speak? I wish it were just that I wasn't familiar with his language but the trouble is he speaks in a language that is non existent on earth.

In spite of his physique favouring the i, Piccirilli's thin and high-pitched voice will only modulate words in which the only vowel is o. Naturally, Piccirilli's voice being so thin, the o sounds like an i. Again, this is a mere conjecture on my part as Piccirilli never pronounced the i, so neither can I affirm that such an o is by comparison really an o or any other vowel.

Applying my scarce knowledge, I have tried to ascertain what language Piccirilli speaks. My attempts have been unsuccessful except that I could establish an invariable succession of vowels and consonants.

This discovery might be of some importance if I was sure Piccirilli actually speaks some language. Any language, regardless of how poor or primitive it is, will show a reasonable extension but the case is that Piccirilli's language is limited to this phrase:

'Dolokotoro povosoro kolovoko.'

I call it a phrase simply for the sake of convenience but who knows what those three words can mean, if they are words and they are three. I transcribe them this way because those are the pauses I seem to perceive in Piccirilli's monotonous elocution.

As far as I know, no European language shows such phonetic features. Concerning African, American or Asian languages, my ignorance is total but that doesn't worry me since, going by his looks, Piccirilli is, like us, of European origin. That's why I addressed him with phrases in Spanish, English, French, Italian and why I even tried phrases in German. Every time Piccirilli's steady little voice replied:

'Dolokotoro povosoro kolovoko.'

Sometimes Piccirilli makes me angry, and other times I feel sorry for him. It is obvious that he laments not being able to make himself understood and so start some conversation with us.

'Us' means my wife and I. The intrusion of Piccirilli did not originate any change in our lives, and the truth is that we are fond of and even love Piccirilli, that minimal musketeer who eats with us in a well-mannered way and who keeps, heaven knows where, a wardrobe and quite a collection of personal objects proportionate to his size.

Even if I can't get him to answer my questions, when we call him Piccirilli he shows no objection to that name. On some occasions, my wife affectionately calls him Pichi. I think this is an excess of familiarity. True, Piccirilli's smallness lends itself to kind nicknames and endearing diminutives. On the other hand, he is an elderly man, perhaps four centuries old, and it would be more proper to call him Mister Piccirilli but it is very difficult to address such a tiny man as Mister.

In general, Piccirilli is a tidy person and his behaviour is exemplary. He sometimes plays with his sword attacking the flies or the ants. Other times, he sits on a toy truck and I, pulling it with a cord, take him for long rides around the flat. Those are his few pleasures.

Does Piccirilli ever get bored? Is he alone in the world? Does he have any fellow beings? Where did he come from? When was he born? Why does he dress as a musketeer? Why is he living with us? What are his aims?

Useless questions repeated hundreds of times to which Piccirilli monotonously replies,

'Dolokotoro povosoro kolovoko.'

There are so many things I would like to know about Piccirilli, so many mysteries that he will carry away the day until he dies.

Because, unfortunately, for several weeks now, Piccirilli has been dying. We were appalled when we learned he was ill and we knew immediately that his case was serious. How to cure him? Who would dare submit to a doctor's judgment the tiny body called Piccirilli? What explanations could we give? How to explain the unexplainable, how to speak about something we did not know?

Yes, Piccirilli is leaving us, and we, submissively, will let him die. I am already thinking about what we will do with his almost intangible body. But I am even more worried, infinitely more worried over not having unravelled a secret that I held in my hands and that I, unable to prevent it, will forever escape me.

EPISODE OF
DON FRANCISCO
FIGUEREDO

(Fragment taken from Dávila, Ramón Enrique, Memorias de un ex legislador, Buenos Aires, Peuser, 1951, pages. 183-191.)

[...]

This doctor Corvalán was a brother of Don Ignacio, in whose villa, at Flores, Rodríguez and Labarthe had taken refuge during the '90s' troubles, an episode I shall deal with more amply in another passage of this book. He was a man of tough build and ruddy face and he kept an affable and cheerful air that made him likeable from the first meeting.

That night, I had the honour of dining at a rotisserie in the centre of town (a restaurant, we would say now) together with my father and doctor Corvalán. I was feeling a little tense and did not partake of the conversation, which was about, what else, politics, except when asked something. After the dinner, my father and doctor Corvalán made their way to the Teatro de la Comedia where I think Sarah Bernhardt, no less, was acting, or perhaps it was Eleonora Duse, and I was sent to rest in my room at the Hôtel des Princes.

But who wanted to sleep? Far from lamenting not being able to go to the theatre with the elders, the adventure of finding myself eight hundred kilometres away from Buenos Aires, having a room all of my own and not lacking a peso in my pocket made me feel immensely happy and in a state close to the intoxication of freedom.

I spent some time leaning on the balcony ledge, enjoying the quietness of the evening and the air full of the scent of orange blossoms and jasmines coming from the neighbouring houses. Some gentlemen wearing their top hats promenaded themselves across the plaza, smoking their cigars. At that time, it was still considered wrong that ladies went to bed late.

I thought it would be a pity to go to sleep and, quite certain that my father would not be annoyed by my disobedience, I decided to go downstairs and take a walk around the unknown town. My father always upheld that a man must learn everything by himself and that he must repeat his mistakes several times before getting things right. The town was not at that time the populous metropolis and striving industrial centre it is today but barely more than a village at whose rail station the local produce arrived.

On the lower ground of the hotel, I saw two modestly dressed women who, judging by the large bags of clothes they were about to pick up, were the hotel's washerwomen. Noticing me, they suddenly went quiet but I had already caught the word chupasangre, and this made me prick my ears. It was the second time in a few hours that I had heard about that matter; before, it had been on the mail coach of the train.

I had learned from my father to gain the trust of all kinds of folks and even then––I must have been fifteen or sixteen—I think I already possessed this gift. So I asked the ladies about this matter of the chupasangre, and their answer indicated that it was one of those vulgar superstitions of our countryside. From what I grasped, the famous chupasangre was a kind of local relative of Count Dracula, the inspirer of the films that came out many more years later.

These ladies told me that in the last few months nine children had died in the town, that the doctors had not been able to identify the cause of their illness, that those children had 'dried up' like a discarded orange. They added that the children must have been 'dried up' by a chupasangre and that a chupasangre, always according to the ladies, was a sufferer of tuberculosis that needed to drink children's blood in order to delay as long as possible his time of death.

Whoever, almost in the middle of the 20th century, reads this nonsensical story will no doubt smile incredulously but these and other like legends were current in the countryside sixty or eighty years ago. And I admit that the ladies, with their timid and fearful air, managed to impart a certain apprehension on me which on the other hand could be attributed, if you like, to my short age and the fact that I felt rather thrilled by being on my own in that so very distant town from Buenos Aires.

The point was that those ladies not only would have sworn to the existence of the chupasangre but also that the owner of such a weird dietary regime had a full name and address known in the area. This belief was not limited to them but was generalised inside the town and in the surrounding farmhouses and even villas.

I remember that when asked to reveal to me the identity of this peculiar individual they looked at each other, frightened, as if hinting that my question, or rather their answer, would jeopardise them.

'You must understand, sir,' one of them said, 'we have small children and if the chupasangre learns that we are accusing him he is going to take revenge on them.'

I promised them I would keep the most absolute secrecy, and, finally, between fussiness and doubts, they told me that the chupasangre was a man called Francisco Figueredo who lived alone in a huge mansion at Belgrano 345 Street, a number very easy to remember indeed.

The house was three or four hundred yards away, and I immediately decided to go and take a look at it. The property occupied an entire block with its main entrance at Belgrano

345 and it had another door, I suppose for the service personnel, at Santa Fe Street. It was entirely surrounded, as it was then the fashion, by iron spear railings. Behind the railings, a garden, looking more like a tangled jungle, and, in the middle of the plot, a large two-story construction imitation of French summer houses although with the unusual presence of a watchtower with glass windows.

All these details, I must have noticed later but on that night I only saw the dark mass of trees and ivies and, beyond, the grey bulk of the building. I would like to here attribute it to my observing or analytical spirit but the truth is that I must have done it out of sheer fright. That time, I watched the estate of Don Francisco from the opposite pavement.

There was only a dim-lit window on the top floor and there, as if within a frame, you could see a really pale--more than pale, totally white--face but with the cheeks sunken to the bone and of a very deep red, the typical face of a consumptive patient.

I stayed several minutes playing the fool, my eyes affixed to the window and on Don Francisco Figueredo's face until he raised his head—from his position, he seemed to be reading-- and then he saw me. That was more than enough for me to pretend that I had just had a passing curiosity and to get away immediately. Out of sheer fright, I almost ran, as a typical kid.

Back in my room, I cursed a thousand times my idea of going downstairs. As soon as I closed my eyes, I saw the white and disapproving face of Don Francisco Figueredo watching me from his lit window. Of course, I was not so naïve as to give credence to those nonsensical stories about the chupasangre but the truth is that I spent a restless night quite propitious to nightmares.

By noon next day, we had already settled in La Dorita, doctor Corvalán's farmhouse. I spent three or four days in awe of the mysteries of the countryside and was already dreaming that such would be my life for ever. I didn't realise that the Fatherland was keeping in reserve for me high responsibilities in public affairs. I was then a boy of about sixteen, raised in Buenos Aires. I was born in Esmeralda Street between Charcas and Paraguay Street. Nevertheless, the Buenos Aires I knew then was wilder and tougher than it is today with so much progress and so many pretensions. But I wanted to say that the countryside appeared to me as a wonderful world where everything was a novelty.

In touch with nature and all noble things created by God, I had almost forgotten the story of the chupasangre. One afternoon, a large crowd was congregated to see my father on account of the political campaign, then in full swing. A man arrived in order to see him and doctor Corvalán. It was the very same Don Francisco Figueredo who was apparently a political player of some importance.

I bumped into him and my father in doctor Corvalán's office waiting room, and so it was necessary to go through the expected introductions and greet him. When my father said, 'Ramón, my eldest son,' and after a pause, 'Don Francisco Figueredo, an old friend,' I blushed to the roots of my hair, thinking that this skinny dry man, an old friend of my father's as he had just said, would recognise me as the impertinent busybody of previous nights. Nonsense, what the hell could he recognise in me if he hadn't even seen me in the shadows of those canopied streets. But I came to this reasoning later.

Anyway, neither he nor my father, urged by matters pertaining to the campaign, noticed my unjustified embarrassment, and I slipped away as best I could.

But apparently I still had not learned my lesson. I felt an odd curiosity and from the court and through the window grills I tried to watch Don Francisco Figueredo three or four times. My father, half-sitting on his desktop, was reading aloud I don't know what political document, and Don

Francisco, sunk but rigid in an armchair, seemed to approve with slight movements the various points submitted for his consideration. Consumption was eating him up, no doubt, and his paleness was truly ghostly, his half-closed eyes emphasizing his cadaverous aspect. Who can tell what class of morbidity led me to pay so much attention to this man who was more dead than alive. Undoubtedly, the vitality of youth is paradoxically attracted to the inanimate and decrepit.

What I did not suspect at that moment was that during the evening of that same day I would be able to observe Don Francisco ad nauseam. He and other recently arrived gentlemen had dinner with us, and, from what I heard, he would be spending the night in La Dorita and would be returning next morning to his house at Belgrano 345.

Perhaps because I was forewarned against him because of the nonsense I had heard from the washerwomen of the hotel, the man certainly gave me an unfavourable impression. Don Francisco hardly spoke and, when he did, his voice sounded muffled and came out with difficulty from his barely opened lips, a truly ghostly voice, I said to myself. I now reflect that, actually, he could not be suffering from consumption because if so, the rest of the gentlemen would not have been eating at his side, fearing, as it was feared, the contagion of that terrible, then incurable, illness.

Two or three times, my eyes met his, which were glassy and had a peculiar and dark fixedness. Not being capable of sustaining that murky sheen, even for an instant, I felt forced to avoid it each time. Finally, I was so overwhelmed by the idea of meeting those inexpressive or too expressive eyes that I no longer dared raise my own from my plate.

A short while later, Juancho Corvalán, doctor Corvalán's fourth son, with whom I sneaked out to have a cigarette—he had initiated me into that habit which luckily I soon gave up— asked me if I, coming from Buenos Aires, believed in vampires.

I suppose he might have been close to his 12th year, and I could boast of two prestige points: being older and a native of the capital.

Of course, with pretentious certainty, I replied that no, I did not believe in vampires. (Even here I showed my awkwardness: I should have first enquired what vampires were and simulate a lack of interest but the truth was that Don Francisco's figure, with his legend, was going around my head).

Afterwards, still feigning indifference, I asked him why he posed that question.

'They say that Don Francisco is a vampire,' the boy answered.

'They say, they say,' I wanted to behave as a sensible mature boy, 'but who says?'

'People, everybody says so.'

'People? What people? Your father says that? My father? The friends of the Party?'

'No, not them but Juliana and the cook and the rest of the servant women...Didn't you see what a strange look he has? His eyes seem to be made out of glass.'

So, he too had noticed it, it wasn't just me.

'...they say he comes out at night and that he has the power of putting the parents to sleep like logs... And then he sucks the children's blood, leaving them dead like a dried-up orange. Or as the spider leaves a fly.'

'Have you any fear?'

'Plenty, to be honest.'

'Lock yourself in.'

'Ha! That would be easy indeed,' he answered mockingly. 'That's it, they say no key or lock will be any good. Don Francisco just gets in.'

'But how does he manage to enter? By breaking the locks?'

'He breaks nothing, he simply gets in, who knows how.'

In front of us was the darkness of the fields with their

tiny odd noises. Behind us, the large illuminated house and, inside, damned Don Francisco with his reptilian look and his ill repute. I started to feel a certain indefinable fear for no sound reason. But I shouldn't be afraid of Juancho who was four years younger than me.

'Don't talk rubbish,' I said, pretending to be unconcerned. 'Let's go and sleep and early tomorrow we could go fishing in the streamlet.'

One way or another, the subject was dropped, and we retired to our rooms. The elders must have stayed up much longer because, after what seemed to me a very long time, I was woken up by the noise of unintelligible voices coming from the hall.

Without lighting the candle, I ran to the window and peeped. It was doctor Corvalán and Don Francisco who were crossing the large inner court toward the bedrooms. Close to my door, they stopped and said good night. Immediately, doctor Corvalán, with his firm and sonorous steps, was lost on the other wing of the building.

I understood that Don Francisco would spend the night in the next room, and that undesirable proximity disturbed me in an irrational manner. I will not bore others with the details and the peculiarities of my insomnia. I will only say that I was scared to death and had a sleepless night. In the countryside, all noises and murmurs are different and have another dimension and a different resonance. I continually seemed to hear veiled moans and something like shoes scratching wood. I found myself several times putting my ear against the wall, trying to decipher the fussy signals I thought I could hear. I had a lump in my throat, and my heart was racing. The fright made me long for my bedroom at Esmeralda Street, in The Retiro, a civilised place where nobody spoke about vampires or chupasangres or any other nonsense.

At some moment, who knows what time it was, I clearly heard Don Francisco's door open. Overcoming the great fear that immobilised my legs, I approached the window and peeped through the net curtains. Don Francisco, with his back to me, was traversing the court toward the pergola where doctor Corvalán habitually drank his mate in the mornings. I recognised him because of his wavering limp and the slope of his weak shoulders; I got the impression that he was carrying a bundle in his arms; this I knew on account of the posture of his body, not because I actually saw it.

I remained still, standing next to the window, in wait of Don Francisco's return. It was a vain wait. Blinded by my anguish and fear, I watched the intangible passing of the night and its slow change into day.

As soon as the day dawned, I dressed and ran outside.

The blue sky, the shining sun, the colours that brightened up, injected the strength in me that I had lacked that dreadful night. Where might Don Francisco be? Where had he spent part of the night?

I crossed the red-tiled court and the gravel path and I reached the pergola. I saw a grill and a few benches and stone tables that were rarely used. Just there, the plains began, interrupted afar by a grove of dark trees. I wondered if Don Francisco, with his sickly countenance, would have been able to walk the several leagues up to the grove.

A dull sound startled me. Something was moving in a corner close to the maleberry hedge. Just in case, I picked up a stick from the floor and I approached it slowly and with much precaution. I saw then a hairy body gasping for breath. I raised the hedge slightly with the stick and I discovered it was a white dog with black ears and a black spot over its right eye. This dog was dying, popeyed, his tongue hanging out. Around his neck, very tightly, it had a cord. Someone had strangled it.

'My God, my God,' I said to myself, shaken with fear. 'My God, I want to go back to Buenos Aires.'

I ran to the house with the intention of telling my father of

Don Francisco's disappearance and the strangling of the dog, no doubt by that hideous man who no one knew where the devil might then be.

One of the maidservants must have noticed something unusual because she asked me, 'Do you need anything, master Ramoncito?'

'My father...Where is my father?'

'With the gentlemen, in the small dining room, drinking mate... Do you need anything, master Ra...?'

Hastily, I ran to the small dining room and entered it abruptly. Surprised, three men looked at me, one was my father, the other, doctor Corvalán and the third one was Don Francisco Figueredo.

I don't know how but I managed to say good morning and gabble some excuse. I then withdrew and went to sit down in a chair in the hall. I needed to reflect and recover my poise.

So, had it all been a dream? Was it the case that the slandered Don Francisco had not abandoned his room for a moment, while I had given way to such absurd ravings?

'Nevertheless,' I thought, 'the strangled dog I didn't see last night. I saw it this morning when I was wide awake and in full sunlight.'

I went back to the pergola, I checked the whole maleberry hedge and I didn't find the white dog with black ears and a black spot over its right eye that I thought I had seen an hour before.

From the farmhouse to the town, a man was approaching on a horse galloping at great haste. I recognised him from afar. It was Antonio, one of the young farmhands that did all kinds of jobs. Without stopping, he shouted, 'I am going to get the doctor! Young Pedrito is dying! The chupasangre has sucked all his blood!'

Pedrito, a lively and pleasant boy, was the son of Juliana, the cook's help. Without losing any time, I went to his sickroom in the servants' quarter. I met with a dramatic picture. On his modest bed, white as a ghost, Pedrito was dying and gibbering. Juliana and other women were crying around him.

'Overnight!' they said. 'Fine yesterday and today he is dying on us! The chupasangre sucked all his blood!'

Suddenly suspicious, they went quiet. My father, doctor Corvalán and Don Francisco Figueredo had just entered the room.

'Calm down, Juliana,' the doctor said. 'Soon, Antonio will be here with the physician, and the kid will be all right.'

My father added some comforting words, and then the three men were out. My head was a pandemonium. The women, now quite openly, started blaming Don Francisco of drinking Pedrito's blood.

'Yesterday, he appeared half-dead and now he looks red and with plenty of health.'

'Yes, red with my poor son's blood!'

What was I doing there? My entire life will not be long enough for me to regret having taken that trip so auspiciously started and now turned into a nightmare. I left the room. I needed to talk with my father and tell him about all my fears.

First, I went to look for Juancho Corvalán.

'Tell me, don't you keep a white dog with black ears and a black spot over its right eye?'

'What do I know? There are so many dogs around here...'

'But try to remember. A dog more or less like this...' Using my hands, I indicated the approximate size, '...with a black spot on its right eye, like a pirate...'

'Oh! yes, you mean the Pirate, Pedrito's dog...!'

'That's the one I mean. Where is it?'

'How do I know? How can I tell where each dog is? It must be around somewhere...'

At that moment, I was called from the hall.

'Master Ramoncito! your father wants you in the small dining room.'

I obeyed instantly; I had the firm intention of talking with my father immediately. This is why I swore to myself when I saw him once again in the dreadful company of Don Francisco Figueredo.

'Don Francisco has been suddenly taken indisposed,' my father said. 'He is returning to his home. He will travel in doctor Corvalán's car. You will accompany him and help him to carry his stuff, which is a bit heavy.'

I looked at Don Francisco. With his neck resting against the chair and his eyes closed, he was breathing with difficulty. I did not see that he was red or 'with plenty of health,' as the women in the kitchen had said. I saw him as white and emaciated as usual.

Justino, a young farmhand of about my age, was tying up the horse to the carriage's shaft. I offered to drive it but my father said, 'No, Justino will travel on the coachman's seat. You will sit with Don Francisco and help him with whatever he may need.'

If, on the one hand, I felt uncomfortable travelling in the coach's box with Don Francisco, on the other, I was happy that Justino was coming with us. During the whole journey, I thought Don Francisco could fall dead there and then. He kept his eyes closed and he was panting laboriously. Every now and then, he moaned and pressed his stomach with his hands. I looked at him implacably. And I did not feel sorry for him.

The damned roads were all flooded with rain. A hundred times we were on the verge of being stranded in the mud, and another hundred the horse managed to overcome the bog.

We finally came to the mansion at Belgrano 345. Justino grabbed Don Francisco's two cases and he tremulously took my arm.

We traversed the wet and derelict garden that I had seen some nights before from the opposite side. With some hesitation, Don Francisco managed to introduce the key in the lock. I felt that characteristic musty smell of the decrepit, typical of houses kept closed for a long time.

'I am feeling ill, very ill,' groaned Don Francisco and he pressed his stomach again.

I tried to help him to get on a sofa but he said, 'No, not in here. I want to get in my bed, upstairs.'

Step by step, we started to climb the stairs. Don Francisco, gasping, held my arm firmly. Justino followed us, carrying the two cases.

We were about to reach the upper hall when, suddenly, Don Francisco suffered some convulsion and fell on top of Justino, which I could not help. Surprised, Justino let go of the cases so he could catch Don Francisco. The cases rolled down the stairs. They tumbled, got beaten, opened up, and, from one of them, the strangled body of Pirate the dog fell out with a muffled sound.

Neither Justino nor I, with our short years, were ready to stand things like that and, screaming heaven knows what words of terror, we ran toward the upper floor. Don Francisco, watching us with hate from the staircase and mumbling some curses, attempted to rise up and pursue us. I can't say what we would have done but I suspect we would have pushed him back down the stairs. But that was not necessary.

Don Francisco broke almost in half, shaking with two new uncontrollable spasms that made him fall flat on his face in the middle of an unending blood vomit. Justino and I stood watching him, not moving. For a long time, the red liquid emanated from his mouth. Every now and then, new contractions increased its volume. After a while, Don Francisco no longer moved, and we understood he had died.

Justino and I made the sign of the cross.

'What a hellish man,' the farmhand said, pointing with his chin to the floor and the bloodied steps. 'It must be Pedrito's.'

There was nothing more to be done in that house. Taking care not to touch the body, we climbed down the stairs.

Justino returned to La Dorita with his fear and his novelties. I did not want to know anything and went back to the Hôtel de Princes. I collected my things and, in a mad rush, I managed to catch the only daily train to Buenos Aires.

Months later, the election campaign having come to an end and the local MP having been chosen, my father returned home. The subject was not mentioned.

This was over seventy years ago, and my father has been dead for forty. When he was still alive I started to know the honours—and why not—also the unpleasantness of holding office. I remember having talked a great deal with my father, touching on almost all imaginable subjects. But I never inquired about Pedrito, and he never asked me about Don Francisco.

ESSENCE AND ATTRIBUTE

On July 25, as I tried to hit letter A, I noticed a slight wart on the pinky of my left hand. On the 27th, it seemed considerably larger. On the third of August, with the help of a jeweller's loupe, I was able to discern its shape. It was a sort of diminutive elephant, the world's smallest elephant, yes, but an elephant complete down to the smallest detail. It was attached to my finger at the end of its little tail. So that, while it was my pinky finger's prisoner, it nevertheless enjoyed freedom of movement except that its locomotion completely depended on my will.

Proudly, fearfully, hesitatingly, I exhibited him to my friends. They were revolted, they said it couldn't be good to have an elephant on one's pinky, they advised me to consult a dermatologist. I scorned their words, I consulted with no one, I had nothing further to do with them, I gave myself over entirely to studying the evolution of the elephant.

Toward the end of August, it was already a handsome little grey elephant the length of my pinky although quite a bit thicker. I played with him all day. At times, I was pleased, to annoy him, to tickle him, to teach him to do somersaults and to jump over tiny obstacles—a match box, a pencil sharpener, an eraser.

At that time, it seemed appropriate to christen him. I thought of several silly and apparently traditional names worthy of an elephant, Dumbo, Jumbo, Yumbo. Finally, I ascetically decided to call him just plain Elephant.

I loved to feed Elephant. I scattered over the table bread crumbs, lettuce leaves, bits of grass. And out there at the edge, a piece of chocolate. Then, Elephant would struggle to get to his treat. But if I held my hand tight, Elephant never could reach it. In this way, I confirmed the fact that Elephant was only a part, the weakest part, of myself.

A short time later when Elephant had acquired the size of a rat, let us say, I could no longer control him so easily. My pinky was too puny to withstand his impetuousness.

At that time, I still was under the misapprehension that the phenomenon consisted solely of Elephant's growth. I was disabused of this idea when Elephant reached the size of a lamb, on that day I too was the size of a lamb.

That night, and a few others too, I slept on my stomach with my left hand protruding from the bed. On the floor beside me, slept Elephant. Afterwards, I had to sleep, face down, my head on his croup, my feet on his back, on top of Elephant. Almost immediately, I found just a portion of his haunch to be sufficient. Afterward, his tail. Afterward, the very tip of his tail where I was only a small wart, totally imperceptible.

At that time, I was afraid I might disappear, cease to be me, be a mere millimetre of Elephant's tail. Later, I lost that fear, I regained my appetite. I learned to feed myself with leftover crumbs, with grains of birdseed, with bits of grass, with almost microscopic insects.

Of course, this was before. Now, I have come to occupy once again a more worthy space on Elephant's tail. True, I am still aleatory. But I can now get hold of an entire biscuit and watch, invisibly, inexpugnably, the visitors to the Zoo.

At this stage of the game, I am very optimistic. I know that Elephant has begun to shrink. As a result, I am filled with an anticipated feeling of superiority by the unconcerned passers by, who toss biscuits to us, believing only in the obvious Elephant they have before them without suspecting that he is no more than a future attribute of the latent essence which still lies in wait.

HABITS OF THE
ARTICHOKE

Very few people are familiar with Ohm Alley. Its only block of any length runs near the corner of Triunvirato and de los Incas avenues. I live in a small balcony apartment facing the inner courtyard.

Even though I am forty eight, I have never felt I would, or could, get married. I manage quite well on my own. My specialty is not agriculture or botany, I teach Spanish, literature and Latin. I don't know anything about those natural rural sciences but I do know a thing or two about linguistics and etymology. It is from these fields that I began my approach to the artichoke.

As you know, a significant percentage of the Spanish lexicon has its origin in the language of the Arab invaders of the eighth century. Sometimes, they would create a word by giving an Arabic form to a Latin or Neo Latin noun that was in current usage in Spain.

Such is the case with the Mozarabic *caucil*, which derives from the Latin *capitiellum*, meaning 'little head.' Thus, *alcaucil* (article + noun) means 'the little head.' This popular name has, shall we say, greater 'expressivity' and 'utility' than the scientific term *Cynara scolymus*. Let us see why.

In Buenos Aires, no one has ever seen an artichoke plant. From the vegetable markets, we are acquainted with specifically those little dead heads whose heart (better said, *receptacle*) and the bases of whose leaves (or rather, *scales*) are certainly very tasty. Well, then, these little heads contain the seed of the flower, and the horticulturist pulls them off the plant before it can develop, as, otherwise, the heads become hard and inedible.

I lived my whole life in complete ignorance of the morphology, life and habits of the artichoke. Now, however, I can say without being pedantic that I have acquired a good deal of information and have become somewhat of an authority on the subject. I am aware, of course, that, regarding the artichoke, much remains to be learned.

The artichoke can be cultivated in a flower pot of generous proportions. Since it is a kind of thistle, a tough hardy plant, it requires little care, it grows quickly. It reaches a height of approximately one metre and, horizontally speaking, a longitude that has until now been impossible to determine.

Although, as a rule, I don't find plants interesting or attractive, I accepted with feigned gratitude the artichoke plant given to me by a neighbour nicknamed Peaches; simple and boring, of a certain age and myopia, she has a son named Sebastian who is rather a dim bulb.

Young Sebas (an apocope favoured by his mother and his friends) had difficulty completing tenth grade. Somehow, I found myself giving him free Spanish lessons so he could attempt to learn in a few days what he had not managed to learn or even suspect in the previous eleven or twelve months.

I don't make any bones about the fact that I am an excellent Spanish teacher with twenty years experience (and weariness) wielding the chalk. But Sebas (hopelessly plebeian and empty-headed) ended up, as I had foreseen, duly flunked by the March examining committee.

Madame Peaches, maternal bias apart, managed to understand that the fault lay not with me but with her son and, in order to thank me in some way, gave me the aforesaid artichoke plant.

Madame Peaches visited my apartment briefly, committed untold errors and half truths as she spoke, paid not the slightest attention to anything I said, conveyed her disillusioned view of the world, and, at last! withdrew, leaving me with the sensation of displeasure that people of low intelligence and boundless ignorance habitually arouse in me. And there on the balcony, the artichoke plant remained, together with a certain ill will, in its red and white flowerpot.

Little by little, it began to propagate a multitude of dull-green heads (artichokes). By their own weight, they pulled down the resisting stems and began to creep along the balcony floor as if they were the many claws of an amorphous unidentifiable animal, a kind of spiny land-octopus with something of the stony green rigidity of prehistoric beasts.

Thus, a week must have passed.

I have spent years vainly fighting the advance of red ants, those invincible omnivorous little insects that occupy an infinite number of caves in my apartment. One afternoon, I happened to be sitting on the balcony; I was reading the newspaper and drinking mate.

And so I observed that four of the many artichoke heads were hunting down red ants. Their strategy was at once simple and efficient. With their scales down and their stems up, they would run like spiders, seize an ant with delicate exactitude and, through rapid traction and mastication, carry it to the centre of the artichoke where it was ingested.

By carefully observing the way the moving stems or tentacles widened at certain points, I could tell that the ants' bodies were transported to the central stem where, I imagined, the digestive apparatus of the artichoke must be located. More than once, I had seen something similar in documentaries. When the snake swallows a mouse or a frog the victim's body can be seen sliding through the body of the executioner, just so did the artichokes eat.

I was elated. This incident seemed auspicious. The artichokes were untiring and insatiable. I realized that, in no time, they would achieve what I had failed to do for years. They would make an end, definitively, of all the red ants in my apartment, those ants that I, in my impotence, so hated.

Indeed, that is what happened. The time came when not a single red ant remained. Then the artichoke began to spread out, looking for other food.

Some artichokes strangled and devoured the other balcony plants—hollyhocks, geraniums, a rosebush that had never flourished, some ancient ferns, a wild spiny cactus. Other artichokes, however, preferred to dig in the ground, capturing useful earthworms and harmful vermin alike. A third group climbed the walls and penetrated the spiders' dark lairs.

Truly, those artichokes had a healthy appetite and they were growing. They were constantly growing. It did not take them long to occupy the whole balcony. Like a climbing vine, they covered the floor, the ceiling, the walls, twisting and turning until they formed an impenetrable jungle.

I must confess, at that point I was a bit scared. I feared stupidly that the plant would continue growing until it occupied the whole apartment.

'Very well,' I told it, 'if that is your intention, I will starve you to death.'

I lowered the grey wooden blinds and hermetically sealed the panes in the dining room and bedroom. I was sure that, deprived of food, the artichoke plant would languish, weaken, shrink and finally wither away in dried up fragments until it died.

I took that precautionary measure Monday, April 11, 1988. Because of some labour dispute or another, classes at my school were suspended toward the end of the week. I took the opportunity to escape briefly to the seaside resort of Mar del Plata, accompanied by a sort of girlfriend, middle aged of course, whom I have been dating for many years, a maths teacher named Liliana Tedeschi. Both train-lovers, averse to buses, we departed from Constitución Station on Wednesday night and subsequently spent three beautiful days in that charming autumnal city.

Sunday, April 17, around eight in the morning, I found myself back in my apartment on Ohm Alley. As I am afraid of thieves, my door is armoured and has two safety bolts. Feeling modestly proud of my foresight, I opened the first bolt, I opened the second, I pushed the door. I noticed that there was a certain amount of resistance, not too much it is true but, in fact, resistance.

Then I entered a kind of artichoke wonderland. I was met by a strong current of air. In my absence, these characters had first eaten up the wooden blinds and then destroyed the window panes. Now, like giant jellyfish, they had scattered throughout the apartment and methodically covered floors, walls and ceilings; they snaked around corners, they scrambled up the furniture, investigated nooks and crannies.

This is what I saw at first glance. I promptly tried to assess the situation more systematically. Although I tried to remain calm, I could not help becoming indignant in the face of such abuses.

The artichokes had opened the refrigerator, the freezer and all the cupboards and had eaten the cheese, the butter, the frozen meats, the potatoes, the tomatoes, the pasta, the rice, the flour, the crackers. Walking across the kitchen, I stumbled over now empty jars of marmalade, olives, pickles, chimichurri sauce.

They had devoured everything that was humanly edible and now, before my enraged eyes, they fell upon everything that was artichokably edible, namely any form of organic matter, dead or alive. And I saw them chewing, clawing and gnawing on the furniture, leather, feathers, wood and all. And I saw them chewing, clawing, and gnawing on the books, oh God! My precious books, lovingly collected over a period of thirty years, the books that I had underlined and annotated, never using ink just pencil, in my neat careful handwriting, not once but a thousand times!

I do not own a butcher knife but I have a pair of scissors for cutting up chickens. I stuck an artichoke stem between the steel blades and, full of hate and joyously malicious, snipped off the enemy's abominable head.

The beheaded artichoke rolled a few centimetres. Instantly, the cut stem branched into countless smaller stems, and simultaneously, fifteen, twenty, fifty new heads were born. Furiously, they threw themselves at me, trying to bite into my shoes, my legs, my hands.

Then, bit by bit, I retreated toward the bathroom and the bedroom. The density of artichokes per square centimetre was much less in this zone. I am a person, I think, who is fairly lucid and I was not inclined to lose my poise. I simply wanted to calm down and think a little, since I did not doubt, I always had great confidence in myself, that I would quickly find a solution to the artichoke problem.

I began to reason.

During my absence, what had exasperated them, even driven them mad? Unquestionably, it was the lack of food. Indeed, during the previous weeks when they had been eating normally, the behaviour of the artichokes had been dignified and judicious. I had only, then, to provide them with the necessary food in order for them to return to their former calm docile selves.

Using the bedroom telephone, there was little left of bed, lamp tables, closets or clothes, I called The Two Friends market. The first friend sells meat, the second friend, fruits and vegetables. From the first, I ordered eight kilos of cheap cuts, liver, lungs, bones. From the second, potatoes and squash, which cost little but yield much. I asked them to deliver it all right away, thus I could satisfy temporarily the artichokes' hunger.

Later, I could seek and would find the definitive solution.

While the artichokes and I waited for the food supplies they continued to gnaw. The noise produced by their gnawing is similar to the sound of a box of matches being shaken with the exception that no one is constantly shaking a box of matches, while, on the other hand, the artichokes were gnawing, gnawing, gnawing the whole time. They continued gnawing on what was left of the furniture; they would swallow up the wood and discard the lacquer and the metallic or plastic elements.

I thought, 'As long as they have something to eat, I will be safe.' And then, immediately, 'What is taking The Two Friends so long?'

Then the doorbell rang (not the intercom buzzer but the bell of the apartment), it rang with that long impatient sound that I abhor. Anticipating my movement, an artichoke pressed the spring lock and opened the door, slowly.

Through the opening, against the darker background of the hallway, wearing a white apron and cap and with an enormous wicker basket carried in both hands, appeared the fat primitive errand boy whom I had seen many times washing down the sidewalk in front of The Two Friends market.

The young man, an enormous twenty year old blockhead weighing close to a hundred kilos, hesitated a moment between greeting me and entering. There was nothing else he could do; in a matter of seconds, he was enfolded by a green web, ductile and efficient, consisting of forty or fifty artichokes. He could not scream or move his arms. With artichokes on his eyes, at his throat and in his mouth, half strangled, and whether alive or already dead I do not know, he was dragged lightly as a feather to the middle of the dining room, and there the artichokes, in a riotous rumble, got down to the task of piercing and eating their way through the fat boy from the market, as well as his wicker basket, the potatoes and squash, the liver, lungs and bones.

That image of the little artichokes running all over his great body reminded me of red ants when they dissect a cockroach, dead or alive.

While these artichokes were ingesting the errand boy, others had locked the apartment door and were now guarding it, far from my reach.

I, therefore, shut myself up in the bathroom, an area that was still devoid of artichokes. I slid the metallic bolt into place, then sat on the edge of the bathtub trying to imagine a quick way to defeat them. With an advanced case of nerves and little time to think, the best plan I could come up with was to start a fire. But, using what? Already, there was hardly anything left that was flammable, my house was just a skeleton of inorganic materials.

This and similar speculation was useless in the end. The best thing, I told myself, is not to think at all. And to wait. Seated on the edge of the bathtub, to wait. Contemplating with stupid attention those familiar objects that were so deprived of interest—the sink, the mirror, the tiles.

The artichokes have already begun gnawing and perforating the bathroom door in twenty different places. Soon, there will be twenty narrow openings and, suddenly, twenty dull green heads advancing toward me.

I am waiting neither resigned nor passive. I have torn out the towel rack and am grasping it like a cudgel. I shall not give up without a fight, I intend to inflict the maximum damage.

I repeat what I said in the beginning, I have learned a great deal but there is still a lot I don't know about the habits of the artichoke.

ILLEGITIMATE AMBITIONS

That the constable aspires to become the Police Commissioner or that the postman dreams of being the Minister of Communication seem to be, and undoubtedly are, far out ambitions. Nevertheless, they imply a desire of betterment and advance, a quality that awakes our sympathy and even our approval.

These are then disproportionate ambitions but there can be no argument that they are legitimate, as legitimate as those of a cat wanting to be a tiger or a hen aspiring to the dignity of an eagle. Those ambitions are of the kind that I am willing to accept, the legitimate ambitions.

In contrast, I refuse to acknowledge and I vigorously reject, for it being illegitimate, absurd, inoperative, the pretension of roaches to become rhinos. I cannot say if the phenomenon is universal. I am only referring to the roaches I find around my home, and, even so, not to all of them but the ones in the little tool shed.

It is true that they have made some progress. Favoured by the last quarter of the moon and the northeast wind, the roaches have begun to approach, how shall I put it, a certain notion of rhinos. Of course, they are still not rhinos and it's very likely that they never will be. But they focus all their physical and mental energies on achieving their ideal, to be rhinos. The roaches are dedicated to that, and all their actions are utilitarian and geared toward reaching it. They don't know about leisure and diversion. They work, struggle and strive in order to be rhinos. I don't think they are much talented but active, hard working and tenacious they certainly are.

Their beginnings were decidedly ridiculous. After growing only a tiny pair of horns over their noses, the roaches attacked little matchboxes, small sticks, paper balls, beverage caps and other similar objects, just as they imagined rhinos did against very voluminous and heavy enemies. I watched them a long time during those practices. I watched them and I smiled. Those exercises, done with such fervour, seemed to me completely ineffective for the roaches to become rhinos. And because of how they concentrated and, because they were so serious, I thought them even more hilarious.

My work and my interests did not always allow me to witness the roaches training. Anyway, the months went by without any worthy sign of progress. I made a note that they are favoured by the conjunction of the last quarter of the moon and the northeast wind.

Only thus can we explain the quick progress of the last few days. The roaches have succeeded in converting their chitin into a pachyderm shield divided into various sections. No longer are they flat, black and shiny but cylindrical, grey and opaque. They have developed a tail and hooves as well as herbivorous habits. Their sight has become much weaker but instead they have increased the sharpness of their sense of smell. They are about twenty centimetres long from nose to rump. Their weight, I estimate to be less than two kilos.

You could almost say that they already are small rhinos. However, the roaches must still attend to some important details. They keep some meanness in their attitudes, some insecurity, some fragility and some ridiculousness. Despite their supposed fierceness and the rhinos' snort they manage to make, they still show a shy and fearful cockroach mentality. When I held one in my arms it desperately shook its six legs in the air and made convulsing movements with its antennae, all of its body shivering in terror.

When I let it go it ran to find refuge in a dark corner under some tins. Unconceivable attitudes in a real rhino. Yes, in spite of their pachyderm shield, their pair of horns over the nose, their voluminous body, their snorts, their short-sightedness, they still are roaches rather than rhinos.

Nevertheless, they look like rhinos. Small rhinos, it's true. Six legged rhinos. Rhinos with long black thread-like antennae. However, rhinos.

I wanted to see if my eyes were deceiving me. Yesterday, I invited the paperboy to see my roaches. These animals appeared a little odd to him, he said, 'they looked like little pigs.' I then told him they were roaches, and he laughed, celebrating my joke.

I now ask myself, when these roaches lose their antennae; when they get rid of a couple of legs; when they remove all the fears that belong to their species; when they reach an imposing size; when they reach a ton; when, in short, they perfect their external rhino identity, who will believe me if I state that those rhinos are roaches?

Above all, how was the illegitimate ambition of turning into rhinos born among the roaches? At some moments, I feel the temptation to grab a broom and exterminate them by beating them on their heads, now when it is still possible to do so. If I abstain from it, it is only because I want to see if the roaches one day succeed in realising their dream of becoming rhinos.

PROBLEM SOLVED

Who hasn't heard of the Insignia Financial Group, a lending institution that underwrites vehicles, agricultural and industrial machinery and, generally, all types of manufacturing products?

I spent three years working at the branch office over in the Parque Patricios neighbourhood located on Avenida Caseros. After I was promoted to a higher position, the company transferred me to the Palermo branch on Avenida Santa Fe. Since I already lived over on Calle Costa Rica just six blocks away, the change worked out very well for me.

Although prohibited by regulations every now and then, we were visited by a few vendors and sales representatives who peddled a variety of articles. Our bosses tended to be lenient and let them in, and so it had become routine practice for the employees to buy things from these people.

This is how I met Boitus, an exceptionally odd person. He was thin as a wire and balding, wore antique style glasses and always dressed in the same grimy threadbare grey suit, all of which gave him the air of a man who had escaped from a silent film era movie. He had a speech defect causing his 'r' to sound like 'd.'

He sold encyclopaedias and dictionaries in instalments and took cash payments for other less costly books. I became one of Boitus' clients because it proved to be a convenient arrangement. I would ask him for a certain book by a certain author, and a few days later Boitus would show up, always reliable, with the book in question, and at the same price as at the local book store.

It didn't take me long to figure out that Boitus was not only extravagant in the way he looked but also in the way he moved and talked. The vocabulary he used was both peculiar and exclusive. When speaking of Juan Pérez, our nation's president, he referred to *Chief What's His Name*. He didn't use the sidewalk but rather *the public walkway*. He didn't ride on the underground rail, microbuses or trains, instead he travelled on *the public passenger transportation system*. He never said, 'I don't know,' it was always, *'I'm unaware'*.

One day as I listened to a certain exchange, I could hardly believe my ears. While at my desk, concentrating on some work related matters, I heard Lucy, one of our most veteran employees on the verge of retiring, ask him, 'Tell me, Boitus, have you ever thought about getting married?'

My curiosity forced me to look up and glance over at Boitus. He broke into a smile that was considerate, perhaps even indulgent.

'Why, my dear Ms. Lucy, there's a simple answer to your question.' He paused for effect. 'I can't marry for three reasons, in the first place, I'm not in an economic position to do so, secondly, I lack the funds and thirdly, I'm broke.'

Boitus' answer and especially the bewildered look on Lucy's face caused me to burst out laughing although I tried my best to contain it. 'Well, well,' I told myself, 'this Boitus guy is quite the comedian.'

I got used to Boitus' periodic visits, during which, besides finalizing book purchases, I was entertained by his eccentricities, paradoxes, logic and outlandish ideas.

He always showed up carrying a brown leather briefcase, so worn that it had become grey, in which he kept invoices, receipts, brochures on encyclopedias, business cards. Anyway, a collection of business related papers, which, God knows why, he generically termed his *judgment tools*. But, besides the briefcase, he always carried five or six packages with him, cardboard boxes filled with books to be delivered.

The day came when our branch manager, Mr. Gatti, an easy going and understanding chap, was promoted and transferred to the head office. His replacement, Mr. Linares, wasn't really a bad person. However, he had a baroque way of speaking, loved circumlocution and was a stickler for rules and regulations. The moment he took over, he laid down the law, and from then on neither Boitus nor any of the other salesmen were allowed over the threshold of the Palermo branch of the Insignia Financial Group.

It was a minor problem, quickly resolved. Boitus and I exchanged phone numbers, and, thus, my purchases and his sales could continue but with one difference. Instead of delivering books to the office, Boitus brought them to my house.

At some point, I realized that I'd now been working at the Palermo branch office a full year and that, consequently, I'd known Boitus for a year and that I bought books from him at fairly regular intervals. But at no point did he ever refer to himself as a 'bookseller.' He called himself a *cultural disseminator*.

The cultural disseminator would arrive at my apartment, weighted down by his dilapidated briefcase, packages and cardboard boxes, to deliver my books, after which he would usually rattle off a string of surprising sophisms, and, after about fifteen minutes, would leave.

I remember well his final visit. Boitus had unleashed an especially strange and extended monologue aimed at instructing me in the use of an absurd taxonomy of his own invention. According to his schema, coffee was a brew, tea was an infusion and boiled mate leaves, a tonic. However, I couldn't get him to explain the grounds for these classifications.

Then, something weird happened. His ideas, which had seemed funny to me at first, suddenly started to irritate me, undoubtedly because of the visceral rejection I feel toward irrationality and error. And, despite suppressing my aggravation, I watched happily as Boitus finally departed with his shabby briefcase and his boxes and packages.

Being that the ground level entrance was permanently locked, I had to follow him down and let him out of the building. Returning to my apartment, I realized Boitus had forgotten one of his parcels on a chair.

It was a round cardboard container, very similar to the ones used to store men's hats. Two green ribbons, originating along its edges but now fallen against each side, functioned as a way to carry the box comfortably.

I removed the lid and, although he couldn't possibly have arrived home yet, I immediately called to inform him of the forgotten merchandise. The phone rang five times before the answering machine picked up. I left a message, the tone of which, polite yet urgent, left no room for doubt.

That night, Boitus did not return my call. The next day, neither. I tried calling and leaving messages for several days at different times.

When I called a week later the phone rang I don't know how many times but neither Boitus nor his answering machine picked up. 'The phone must be disconnected,' I told myself.

A few hours later, my calls were answered by a female voice that recited, 'The number you have dialled does not belong to any client within the Telecom network.' A while later, dialling Boitus' number produced nothing but silence, as though both the number and the phone itself had disappeared.

At the office, I mentioned all this to Rossi whose desk adjoins mine, and he offered to come over to my place.

'As long as it isn't a bother,' he added.

'Quite the opposite,' I said, 'I'd appreciate your help.'

And so it happened that, having finished our workday, Rossi visited my apartment for the first and last time. Opening the box, he drew back with a distasteful look on his face.

'Oh dear, looks like this is going to be complicated.'

'Definitely, can't say I didn't warn you.'

Then, Rossi completely lost interest in the box and became distracted as he looked around. In a matter of seconds, he had me feeling nervous. He's a restless man and started walking the length of the apartment offering different criticisms or suggestions which I had never asked for, such as, 'This would be a good place to hang a mirror,' or 'Aren't your doors sealed against draughts? There seems to be air getting in.'

He stopped in front of a framed picture of Cecilia Capelli, picked it up for a moment, put it back down in a slightly different location and then commented, 'So this is your girlfriend? Cute girl, congratulations.'

I told myself that he could have dispensed with both his remark and the congratulations. My love affair with Cecilia was in a state of deterioration, and several times I had been tempted to get rid of the picture since its presence only served to upset me.

He then inspected my library and seized the opportunity to ask to borrow *A History Of Argentinean Soccer*. I detest lending books (or borrowing them, for that matter) but as he had been so kind as to come over and help me, I couldn't say no.

I had ascertained that Rossi was restless. A few days later, I found out that in addition he tended to talk too much. Consequently, on Friday, Mr. Linares called me to his office and closed the door after I'd entered. Through the intercom he commanded, 'Flavia, no calls until further notice.'

He had me sit facing him over his desk and then, with a smile that was intended to look congenial but was obviously forced, he told me, 'My dear Sainz, it's not that I want to involve myself in something that's none of my business but in a certain way, you being a young man of twenty eight, relatively new to the company, and seeing how...'

I'm about to be heaved down into the labyrinth of his meandering prose, I thought.

'I'm somewhat older with more years under my belt and your manager on top of that, a kind of father figure within the company you could say; I have a kind of, how should I put it, moral obligation to help you. Am I right?'

Since Mr. Linares was waiting for an answer, I immediately agreed, motivated by the desire to get him to stop talking as soon as humanly possible.

'Well then,' he continued, 'if it is acceptable to you, tomorrow, which is Saturday and will give us some free time, I'll take a little jaunt over to your house to see what we can do.'

I had no choice but to accept his offer. Back at my desk, Rossi avoided eye contact. However, a few minutes later, he approached me and muttered in my ear, 'Don't think I'm the one who told him about it. He already knew. It's hard to hide these things.'

I wondered how Rossi knew that Linares had found out.

On Saturday, I had to get up early. I couldn't have Mr. Linares over to a typical bachelor's apartment that hadn't been cleaned in at least two weeks. I spent most of my morning on detestable chores, vacuuming the floor, dusting the furniture, cleaning the bathroom and kitchen. Finally, by 11am, my house was in a presentable state for receiving Mr. Linares.

When he showed up he wasn't alone. With him were Araujo, our office errand boy, who was fond of gambling, and another gentleman I had never met who wore a suit, tie and spectacles.

'Dr. Venancio,' said Linares, introducing him. 'He's a legal representative or, if you prefer, an attorney who will certify the affidavit. As for Araujo,' he added affably, 'he needs no introduction. Who doesn't owe Araujo a favour or two, right?'

Araujo, dressed in his office uniform, smiled shyly.

'Araujo is only here as a witness, so that Dr. Venancio can get his signature on the affidavit.'

'Fine,' I said. 'Sounds good.'

Mr. Linares took the lid off the box and, holding the lid in his right hand, carefully examined the contents. Dr. Venancio and Araujo immediately did the same.

'Everything in order, Araujo?' Mr. Linares asked.

'Yes, sir, no problem.'

Dr. Venancio spread the affidavit out on the dining room table. It was three pages long. He signed his name in the margins of the first two and at the bottom of the third. Then, he turned to Araujo and indicated he should do the same. Araujo signed slowly, it was obvious he was not very seasoned at working with papers and documents.

'Should I sign?' I asked.

'It's not necessary,' replied the public notary, 'but it isn't prohibited, either. It's up to you.'

'I'm going to sign just in case.'

I took a moment to read the affidavit and confirmed that it rigorously conformed to the truth. Then I signed it.

'And you, Mr. Linares? Would you like to sign?'

'No, Doctor, it doesn't appear to be necessary or even prudent.'

After exchanging a few platitudes about the weather, my visitors left.

I had planned to go to the movies that night with Cecilia but around six in the evening she called to cancel the date.

'The problem is my father,' she explained. 'Well, that is, if you want to call it a problem. I don't think there's any reason for concern but he does. He thinks that your situation might affect his chances of getting elected mayor.'

I felt like telling her to go to hell, along with her distinguished father, a power hungry political schemer but I held back and only said, 'Fine, sounds good.'

I thought it's just as well, I'm fed up with her.

I looked up Boitus' telephone number using a directory on the Internet and found out he lived on Calle Fraga in the Chacarita neighbourhood. On Sunday morning, I headed over to the house in question. There, I found a wooden barrier around the building with a sign that read, NOTICE: BUILDING TO BE COMPLETELY DEMOLISHED. NEW CONSTRUCTION OF ONE AND TWO BEDROOM APARTMENTS.

With the exception of a few unexpected events, my life continued its normal path.

It wasn't long before I was given another promotion that entailed one advantage and one drawback. The former involved a substantial salary increase; suddenly, I was earning practically double what I had been up to now (which already was no small sum). The drawback resided in that I had to carry out my new duties in the suburb of Béccar, quite a distance from my place on Calle Costa Rica.

I added up the pros and cons and, after finally accepting the promotion, resigned myself to a long commute between Palermo and my new destination. The ideal situation would have been to buy a place in Béccar or in San Isidro but to come up with the money I first would have had to sell the apartment on Calle Costa Rica.

Without meaning to, I had also gained a certain notoriety and I discovered that having it wasn't all that bad. Photographers and feature writers showed up from the newspapers *La Nación* and *Clarín* and from the magazines *Caras* and *Gente*. I was subjected to interviews and was photographed, now smiling, now solemn, next to the round box. I was also invited to talk on television news programmes, something I did with some degree of vanity. I didn't even turn down invitations to appear on frivolous talk shows filled with gossip and tabloid stories.

In the end, 'Doctor' Ignacio Capelli didn't succeed in being elected mayor of Tres de Febrero County, a fact that pleased me no end. At this point, I had had it with Cecilia, so a few days later I found a random excuse to break up with her.

On the other hand, something wonderful had happened. I had gotten into the habit of having an afternoon snack after work at a café near Béccar station. At the same time of day, several teachers from a nearby school would come by after finishing with their classes. They were lovely girls who spoke loudly and always roared with laughter.

I was attracted to one of them (I already knew her name, Guillermina), and more than once our eyes, her's a crystal blue, met across the tables. One day, as I was leaving, I arranged for an 'accidental' meeting out on the sidewalk and was able to strike up a conversation. Straight away, I accompanied her home, first by train until we reached the Belgrano neighbourhood, then by foot a few blocks. She was twenty five years old, her name was Guillermina Grotz and she still lived with her parents.

Things went well, and it didn't take me long to become her boyfriend and, a few weeks later, begin intimate relations.

One afternoon, as we lay on a hotel bed, she asked me, 'Wouldn't it be cheaper for you to invite me to your apartment?'

Surprised, I looked her in the eyes. 'Aren't you aware of the problem I have?'

'How could I not know? Everybody knows about it. But it can't be all that bad.'

The generosity I saw in her eyes moved me. I felt a tear welling up but quickly wiped it away.

The following Saturday, I took Guillermina out to a movie in Belgrano. Afterward, I treated her to dinner at a restaurant on Avenida Cabildo.

'Well,' I told her, 'now we're going back to my place to end the night on a dignified note.'

As we entered the apartment and I turned on the light,

Guillermina cried out, 'At last, I get to see Mr. Sainz's mysterious bunker!'

But before she had a chance to get to know the place, she stopped in front of the round box. She hesitated for a moment and then lifted the lid. The expression on her face didn't change one bit but she said, 'You were right. We should go back to what we were doing before.'

I wanted her to define her terms, so I asked, 'Should we go to the bedroom or do you want to leave?'

'I hope I don't offend you but I prefer to leave.'

'Why should I be offended? You're completely within your rights.'

Guillermina lived near the corner of Cuba and Mendoza. I stopped a taxi coming down the street and bid her farewell.

But not for good, there was no reason we should break up. On the contrary, the experience had drawn us closer together.

Three months later, we were married and went to live in a tiny apartment we had rented outside the city, in San Isidro, a place that was soon crammed with all the belongings Guillermina and I had brought from our respective former homes. My dining room set consisted of a table and four chairs but I could only bring three of the four to San Isidro.

At my workplace, I was subjected to questions that were as naïve as they were predictable and, as well, faced some slightly troublesome bureaucratic snags, none of which kept me from continuing to rise in the company.

In fact, I'd say that in this regard I couldn't complain. Each new success brought me a higher position, and I continued to climb the hierarchical ladder and earn more money.

One Friday afternoon (the best moment of the week), I was summoned to the head office. No less than the senior director himself offered congratulations and assured me that without a shadow of a doubt, within the year, I would be named manager of the Mar del Plata branch office.

'So, Mr. Sainz, it would be best for you to begin getting your affairs in order ahead of time.'

Mar del Plata is a magnificent assignment although being so far down the coast it will mean Guillermina has to resign her teaching position and the two of us will have to move. Once there, it won't be hard for my wife to get a job at another school.

Guillermina and I have become frugal to the point of greediness. We want to have enough money to buy a relatively spacious apartment in Mar del Plata, and I believe we will. The only possible way is to save and save and save since we can't count on the money we would get from the impossible sale of my former residence on Calle Costa Rica, which, by the way, had all the utilities cut off, electricity, telephone, gas, water. I also stopped paying the building maintenance fees and the municipal taxes.

'They're going to take you to court and foreclose on the apartment,' Guillermina often comments.

Without fail I answer, 'But they'll never find a buyer.'

'That's true,' Guillermina always replies in turn, 'but it's not our problem.'

REWARDING
SUPERSTITIONS

I live on the superstitions of others. I don't earn much, and the work is pretty hard.

My first job was in a seltzer plant. The boss believed, who can say why, that one of the thousands of siphon bottles (yes, but which one?) harboured the atomic bomb. He also believed that the presence of a human being was enough to prevent that fearful energy from being released. There were several of us employees, one for each truck. My task consisted of remaining seated on the irregular surface of the siphon bottles during the daily six hours required in the distribution of the seltzer. An arduous task, the truck jolted, the seat was uncomfortable, painful, and the route was boring. The truckers, a common lot; every once in a while a siphon bottle would explode (not the one with the atomic bomb) and I would sustain slight injuries. Finally, tired of it, I quit. The boss hastened to replace me with another man who with his mere presence would prevent the explosion of the atomic bomb.

I immediately learned that a spinster lady in Belgrano had a pair of turtles and she believed, who can say why, that one of them (yes, but which one?) was the Devil in the form of a turtle. Since the lady, who always wore black and said her rosary, couldn't watch them continually, she hired me to do so at night.

'As every one knows,' she explained to me, 'one of these two turtles is the Devil. When you see one of them begin to sprout a pair of dragon wings don't fail to inform me because that's the one, without a doubt, who is the Devil. Then we'll make a bonfire and burn it alive so as to make all evil disappear from the face of the earth.'

I stayed awake during the first nights, keeping an eye on the turtles, what stupid clumsy animals. Later, I felt my zeal to be unjustified and, just as soon as the spinster lady would go to bed, I would wrap my legs in a blanket and, curled up in a folding chair, I would sleep away the entire night. So, I never managed to discover which of the two turtles was the Devil. Later, I told the lady that I was going to give up that job because it seemed it was bad for my health to stay awake all night.

Besides, I had just learned that there was an old mansion in San Isidro overlooking a deep ravine and, in the mansion, a statuette depicting a sweet French girl of the end of the nineteenth century. The owners, a very old grey haired couple, believed, who can say why, that that girl was sad and pining for love and that if she didn't get a beau she would die in a short time. They provided me with a salary, and I became the statuette's boyfriend. I began to call on her. The old folks left us to ourselves, though I suspect they spied on us. The girl receives me in the gloomy parlour, we sit on a worn sofa, I bring her flowers, bon bons or books, I write poems and letters to her, she languidly plays the piano, she glances at me tenderly. I call her 'my Love,' I furtively kiss her, at times I go beyond what is permitted by the decorum and innocence of a late nineteenth century girl.

Giselle loves me too, she lowers her eyes, slightly sighs and says to me, 'When will we be married?'

'Soon,' I answer. 'I'm saving up.'

Yes but I keep putting off the date since I can't save more than a little towards our wedding. As I've already said, you don't earn very much living on other people's superstitions.

THE CUBELLI LAGOON

In the south-east region of the provincial plains of Buenos Aires, you might come across the Cubelli Lagoon, familiarly known as the 'Lake of the Dancing Alligator.' This popular name is expressive and graphic but, just as Doctor Ludwig Boitus established, it is inaccurate.

In the first place, 'lagoon' and 'lake' are distinct hydrographic occurrences. Secondly, though the alligator, *Caiman yacare* (Daudin), of the *Alligatoridae* family, is common to America, this lagoon is not the habitat for any species of alligator.

Its waters are extremely salty and its fauna and flora are what you would expect for creatures that inhabit the sea. For this reason, it cannot be considered unusual that in this lagoon a population of approximately one hundred and thirty marine crocodiles are to be found.

The 'marine crocodile', that is the *Crocodilus porosus* (Schneider), is the largest of all living reptiles. It commonly reaches a length of some seven metres (twenty three feet), weighing more than a ton. Doctor Boitus affirms to having seen along the coasts of Malaysia several of them that were over nine metres (thirty feet) in length and, in fact, has taken and brought back photographs that supposedly prove the existence of such large individuals. But, as they were photographed in marine waters without external points of reference, it is not possible to determine precisely if those crocodiles were truly the size attributed to them by Doctor Boitus. It would of course be absurd to doubt the word of an investigator with such a brilliant career (even though his language is rather baroque) but scientific rigour requires that the facts be validated by inflexible methods that, in this case, were not put to use.

Well then, it happens that the crocodiles of the Cubelli Lagoon possess exactly the taxonomic characteristics of those that live in the waters around India, China and Malaysia, hence, they should by all rights be called marine crocodiles or *Crocodili porosi*. However, there are some differences, which Doctor Boitus has divided into *morphological traits* and *ethological traits*.

Among the former, the most important (or, better said, the only) is size. Whereas the marine crocodile of Asia can be up to seven metres long, the one we have in the Cubelli Lagoon scarcely reaches, in the best of cases, two metres (six feet six inches), measuring from the tip of the snout to the tip of the tail.

Regarding its ethology, this crocodile is 'fond of musically harmonized movements' according to Boitus (or, to use the simpler term preferred by those in the town of Cubelli, 'dancing'). As anyone knows, as long as crocodiles are on land they are as harmless as a flock of pigeons. They can only hunt and kill when in the water, which is their vital element. They trap their prey between their toothy jaws, then rotate rapidly, spinning until their victim is dead. Their teeth have no masticatory function being designed exclusively to imprison and swallow a victim whole.

If we go to the shores of the Cubelli Lagoon and start to play music, having previously chosen something appropriate for dancing, right away we will see that, let's not say all, almost all the crocodiles rise out of the water and, once on land, begin to dance to the beat of the tune in question.

For such anatomical and behavioural reasons, this saurian has received the name *Crocodilus pusillus saltator* (Boitus).

Their tastes are varied and eclectic, and they do not seem to distinguish between aesthetically worthy music and music of little merit. Popular tunes delight them no less than symphonic compositions for ballet.

These crocodiles dance in an upright position, balancing only on their hind legs, reaching an average height of one metre, seventy centimeters (5 feet 8 inches). In order not to drag on the ground, their tails rise at an acute angle, roughly parallel to their spines. At the same time, their front limbs (which we could well call hands) follow the beat with various amusing gestures while their yellow teeth form a wide smile exuding enthusiasm and satisfaction.

Some townspeople are not in the least attracted by the idea of dancing with crocodiles but many others do not share this aversion. It's a fact, every Saturday when the sun goes down they put on their party clothes and gather on the shore of the lagoon. There the Cubelli Social Club has set up everything necessary to make the evening unforgettable. Likewise, people can dine in the restaurant that has arisen not far from the dance floor.

The arms of the crocodile are rather short and cannot embrace the body of their partner. The gentleman or lady dancing with the male or female crocodile that has chosen them places both hands on one of their partner's shoulders. To achieve this, one's arms must be stretched to the maximum at a certain distance. As the snout of a crocodile is quite pronounced, one must take the precaution of standing as far back as possible. Though disagreeable episodes have occasionally occurred (such as nasal excision, explosion of ocular globes, or decapitation), it must not be forgotten that, as their teeth may contain the remains of cadavres, the breath of this reptile is far from being attractive.

According to Cubellian legend, occupying the small island in the centre of the lagoon are the king and queen of the crocodiles who it seems have never left it. They say they are each more than two centuries old and, perhaps owing to their advanced age, perhaps owing simply to whim, they have never wished to participate in the dances organized by the Social Club.

The get togethers do not last much past midnight for at that hour the crocodiles begin to tire and maybe get a little bored. In addition, they feel hungry and, as their access to the restaurant is prohibited, they want to return to the water in search of food.

When no more crocodiles remain on terra firma the ladies and gentlemen go back to town, rather tired and a little sad but with the hope that, maybe at the next dance, or perhaps at a later one, the crocodiles' king or the queen or even both together might abandon their island for a few hours and participate in the party. If this were to happen, each gentleman, though he takes care not to show it, harbours the illusion that the queen of the crocodiles will choose him for her dance partner. The same is true of all the ladies who dream of dancing with the king.

THE EMPIRE OF
THE COTORRITAS

Ordinary people in Argentina have never heard of the *Cicadella viridis*. This is the scientific name given to those small hemiptera, quite harmless and of very short life, that in summer evenings gyrate around lamps. Instead, no doubt due to an association of ideas because of their green colour, they call them by the popular term of *cotorritas* (equivalent to the English 'parakeets').

Their movements do not appear to be governed by intelligent thought. Lacking the fly's sharp sight and rapid reactions, the nuisance is easily eliminated by crushing them between the thumb and index finger. In contrast to the mosquito, they are incapable of biting. Nevertheless, they are sheer torment for anyone trying to read or eat. They throw themselves blindly against your face or eyes, they drown in your soup, they smudge your writing. By the time you manage to brush aside the five or six *cotorritas* walking on your fork, another ten or twelve are already in your ears or up your nose.

Why should these tiny green hemiptera, the *cotorritas*, be so stupid, so feeble-minded? Their behaviour is perhaps the least sensible of any living thing. Those who believe that this behaviour is common to all insects are wrong. For instance, a man can establish with a cockroach a kind of relationship, if not friendly then logical at least. The man will attempt to kill the cockroach, which will try to run away and hide. This is simply not possible with the *cotorritas*. No one knows what they are doing or why they are doing it.

'But,' asks Dr. Ludwig Boitus himself in one of his latest papers, 'is the *cotorritas'* behaviour really so mad? Let us start from the premise that all living beings orientate their actions towards the preservation of their species. Why should the *cotorritas'* behaviour be an exception to such sound, well-proven law? [...]. The modern researcher,' he adds, 'must not limit himself to simple statements to the effect that the *cotorritas'* actions are gratuitous and senseless. He should make an effort to determine the true logic behind the apparently absurd illogical behaviour of the *cotorritas*. This behaviour is merely an outward expression of an inner motivation, and it is time we found out what that might be.*

Dr. Boitus mentions two facts that have generally been ignored. Firstly, in recent times it has been observed that the *cotorritas* fly less around lights than around people's heads and, secondly, their numbers are increasing. He points out that, although the *cotorritas* seem to lack even a minimal offensive or defensive weapon, five hundred or a thousand of them, by continually harassing a man, entering his ears and eyes, walking on his neck, stopping him from thinking, reading, writing or sleeping, can force him, in fact, do force him, into a state of complete mental derangement. In this state, it is the man not the parakeet who does not know what he is doing or why he is doing it. It is a state in which the man does not even know who he is and when he enters it, when he loses consciousness of his own self, he inevitably becomes resigned to being surrounded and dominated by the *cotorritas*. Furthermore, from that moment on, he can no longer live without the *cotorritas*, without feeling them inside his ears, his eyes and his mouth. What has occurred is a phenomenon that 'in the field of drug addiction is known as dependency. And this,' Boitus adds, 'is the true purpose of the *cotorritas*,

---

* Boitus, Ludwig: "Función de la conducta de los insectos en la preservación de la especie", in *Anales del Mundo Contemporáneo*, XXXIV, 158, La Plata, University of La Plata, January-February, 1973.

the underlying logic behind their apparently absurd and illogical behaviour.'

The *cotorritas* are inexorably expanding their empire. To date, they have taken over every civilized country. The more advanced a nation's technology, the stronger their hold. Wherever there is electric light, the *cotorritas* reign supreme.

On this point, a world atlas accompanying the article shows how few countries are still free of the Empire of the *Cotorritas*. However, we believe that the inclusion of this map is a fallacy. This is not a political empire. *Cotorritas* rule only over minds. When these have been *cotorrizadas* ('parakeetised'), to use the neologism coined by Boitus, they go on to *cotorrizan* ('parakeetise') the bodies, which consequently begin to perform essentially *cotorríticas* ('parakeetic') actions. As Dr. Boitus concludes, 'At this point, only primitive communities and the poorest countries remain almost free of *cotorritas*, countries untouched by the development of mass media.'

THE LIBRARY
OF MABEL

1

As the sufferer of a certain classificatory mania, from my adolescence I took the care of cataloguing the books in my library.

By my fifth year of secondary school, I already possessed a reasonable, for my age, number of books: I was approaching six hundred volumes.

I had a rubber stamp with the following legend:

Library of Fernando Sorrentino
Volume n° _____
Registered on: _____

As soon as a new book arrived, I stamped it, always using black ink, on its first page. I gave it its corresponding number, always using blue ink, and wrote its date of acquisition. Then, imitating the old National Library's catalogue, I entered its details on an index card which I filed by alphabetical order.

My sources of literary information were the editorial catalogues and the *Pequeño Larousse Ilustrado*. An example at random: in some collections from the various editors were *Atala, René, El último abencerraje*. Sparked by such profusion and because Chateaubriand on the pages of the Larousse seemed to have a great importance, I acquired the book in the edition of Colección Austral from Espasa-Calpe.

In spite of these precautions, those three stories turned out to be unbearable to me as they were so evanescent.

In contrast with these failures, there were also total successes. In the Robin Hood collection, I was fascinated by *David Copperfield* and, in the Biblioteca Mundial Sopena by *Crimen y castigo.*

Along the even-numbered side of Santa Fe Avenue, a short distance from Emilio Ravignani Street was the half-hidden Muñoz bookshop. It was dark, deep, humid and mouldy with wooden creaking planks. Its owner was a Spanish man about sixty years old, very serious and somewhat haggard.

The only one sales assistant was the person who used to serve me. He was young, bold and prone to errors and without much knowledge of the books he was asked about nor where they were located. His name was Horacio. At the moment I entered the premises that afternoon, Horacio was rummaging around some shelves looking for heaven knows what title. I managed to learn that a tall and thin girl had enquired about it. She was, in the meantime, glancing at the wide table where the second hand books were exhibited.

From the depths of the shop, the owner's voice was heard:

'What are you looking for now, Horacio?'

The adverb *now* showed some bad mood.

'I can't find *Don Segundo Sombra,* don Antonio. It is not on the Emecé shelves.'

'It is a Losada book, not Emecé, look on the shelves of the Contemporánea.'

Horacio changed the location of his search and, after a great deal of exploration, he turned toward the girl and said to her:

'No, I am sorry; we have no *Don Segundo* left.'

The girl lamented the fact, said she needed it for school and asked where she could find it.

Horacio, embarrassed before an unfathomable enigma, opened his eyes widely and raised his eyebrows.

Luckily, don Antonio had overheard the question:

'Around here,' he answered, 'it is very hard. There are no good bookshops. You will have to go to the centre of town, to El Ateneo or some other in Florida o Corrientes. Or perhaps near Cabildo and Juramento.'

Disappointment upset the girl's face.

'Forgive me for barging in,' I said to her. 'If you promise to take care of it and return it to me, I can lend you *Don Segundo Sombra.*'

I felt as if I was blushing, as if I had been inconceivably audacious. At the same time, I felt annoyed with myself for having given way to an impulse that was contrary to my real feeling. I love my books and hate lending them.

I don't know what exactly the girl answered but after some squeamishness she ended up accepting my offer.

'I have to read it immediately for school,' she explained, as if to justify herself.

I then learnt that she was in the third year in the women's college at calle Carranza. I suggested that she accompanied me home and I would let her have the book. I gave her my full name, and she gave me hers. She was called Mabel Mogabaru.

Before starting our journey, I accomplished what had taken me to the Muñoz bookshop. I bought *Los crímenes de la rue Morgue.* I had already the *Historias extraordinarias* and, with much delight, decided to dwell once again on the fiction of Edgar Allan Poe.

'I don't like him at all,' Mabel said. 'He is gruesome and full of effect, always with those stories of murders, of dead people, of coffins. Cadavers don't appeal to me.'

While we walked along Carranza toward Costa Rica Street, Mabel spoke full of enthusism and honesty about her interest in or, rather, passion for literature. On that point, there was a deep affinity between us but, of course, she mentioned authors who converged in and diverged from our respective literary loves. Although I was two years older than her, it seemed to me that Mabel had read considerably more books than me.

She was a brunette, taller and thinner than what I had thought in the bookshop. A certain diffused elegance adorned her. The olive shade of her face seemed to mitigate some deeper paleness. The dark eyes were fixed straight on mine, and I found it hard to withstand the intensity of that steady stare.

We arrived at my door in Costa Rica Street.

'Wait for me on the pavement; I'll bring you the book right away.'

And I did find the book instantly as, because of a question of homogeneity, I had (and still have) my books grouped by collection. Thus, *Don Segundo Sombra* (Biblioteca Contemporánea, Editorial Losada) was placed between Kafka's *Metamorfosis* and Chesterton's *El candor del padre Brown*.

Back in the street, I noticed, although I know nothing about clothes, that Mabel was dressed in a somewhat, shall we say, old-fashioned style with a greyish blouse and black skirt.

'As you can see,' I told her, 'this book looks brand new, as if I had just bought it a second ago in don Antonio's bookshop. Please take care of it, put a cover on it, don't fold the pages as a marker and, especially, don't even think of writing a single comma on it.'

She took the book—with such long and beautiful hands— with what I thought was a certain mocking respect. The volume, of an impeccable orange colour, looked as if it had just left the press. She turned the pages for a while.

'But I see that you do write on books,' she said.

'Certainly, but I use a pencil, with a small and very meticulous writing, those are notes and useful observations for enriching my reading. Besides,' I added, slightly irritated, 'the book belongs to me, and I give it any use I like.'

I immediately regretted my rude remark, as I saw mortification in Mabel's face.

'Well, if you don't trust me, I prefer not to borrow it.'

And she handed it back to me.

'No, not at all, just take care of it, I trust your wisdom.'

'Oh,' she was looking at the first page. 'You have your books classified?'

And she read in loud voice, not jokingly:

'Library of Fernando Sorrentino. Volume number 232. Registered on: 23/04/1957.'

'That's right, I bought it when I was in the second year of secondary. The teacher requested it for our work in Spanish Lit classes.'

'I found the few short stories I've read by Güiraldes rather poor. That's why I never thought of getting *Don Segundo*.'

'I think you are going to like it, at least there are no coffins or cursed houses or people buried alive. When do you think you'll be returning it?'

'You'll have it back within a fortnight, as radiant'—she emphasised—'as you are giving it to me now. And to make you feel more relaxed, I am writing my address and telephone number.'

'That's not necessary,' I said out of decorum.

She took out a ballpoint pen and a school notebook from her purse and wrote something on the last page, and I accepted it. To be sure, I gave her my telephone number, too.

'Well, I am very grateful...I am going home now.'

She shook my hand (no kisses at that time as is the way now) and she walked toward the Bonpland corner.

I felt some discomfort. Had I made a mistake by lending a book dear to me to a completely unknown person? The information she had given me, could it be apocryphal?

The page in the notebook was squared; the ink, green. I searched the phonebook for the name Mogaburu. I sighed with relief, a MOGABURU, HONORIO was listed next to the address written by Mabel.

I placed a card between *Metamorfosis* and *El candor del padre Brown* with the legend '*Don Segundo Sombra*, missing, lent to Mabel Mogaburu on Tuesday 7th of June 1960. She promised to return it, at the latest, on Wednesday 22nd of June.' Under it, I added her address and phone number.

Then, on the page of my agenda for the 22nd of June, I wrote: 'Mabel. Attn! *Don Segundo*.'

2

That week and the next went by. I continued with my usual, mostly unwanted, activities as a student in my last year of secondary.

We were on the afternoon of Thursday the 23rd. As it usually happens to me, even to this day, I make annotations on my agenda that I later forget to read. Mabel had not called me to return the book or, if that was the case, to ask me to extend the loan.

I dialled Honorio Mogaburu's number. At the other end, the bell rang up to ten times but nobody answered. I hung up the phone but called again many times, at different times, with the same fruitless result.

The process was repeated on Friday afternoon.

Saturday morning, I went to Mabel's home on calle Arévalo between Guatemala and Paraguay.

Before ringing the bell, I watched the house from across the street. A typical Palermo Viejo construction, the door in the middle of the facade and a window on each side. I could see some light through one of them. Would Mabel be in that, a room occupied with her reading...?

A tall dark man opened the door. I imagined he must be

Mabel's grandfather.

'What can I do for you...?

'I beg your pardon. Is this Mabel Mogaburu's home?'

'Yes but she is not here right now. I am her father. What did you want her for? Is it something urgent?'

'No, it's nothing urgent or very important. I had lent her a book and...well, I am needing it now for...'—I searched for a reason—'a test I have on Monday.'

'Come in, please.

Beyond the hallway, there was a small living room that appeared poor and old-fashioned to me. A certain unpleasant smell of stale tomato sauce mixed with insecticide vapours floated in the air. On a small side table, I could see the newspaper *La Prensa*, and there was a copy of *Mecánica Popular*.

The man moved extremely slowly. He had a strong resemblance to Mabel, he had the same olive skin and hard stare.

'What book did you lend her?'

'*Don Segundo Sombra*.'

'Let's go into Mabel's room and see if we can find it.'

I felt a little ashamed for troubling this elderly man that I judged unfortunate and who lived in such sad house.

'Don't bother,' I told him. 'I can return some other day when Mabel is here, there is no rush.'

'But didn't you say that you needed it for Monday...?'

He was right, so I chose not to add anything.

Mabel's bed was covered with an embroidered quilt of a mitigated shine.

He took me to a tiny bookcase with only three shelves.

'These are Mabel's books. See if you can find the one you want.'

I don't think there were one hundred books there. There were many from Editorial Tor among which I recognized, because I too had that edition from 1944, *El fantasma de la Opéra* with its dreadful cover picture. And I identified other common titles, always in rather old editions.

But *Don Segundo* wasn't there.

'I took you into the room so you could stay calm,' said the man. 'But Mabel hasn't brought books for many years to this library. You have seen that these are pretty old, right?'

'Yes, I was surprised not to see more recent books...'

'If you agree and have the time and the inclination,' he fixed his eyes on me and made me lower mine, 'we can settle this matter right now. Let's look for your book in Mabel's library.'

He put on his glasses and shook a key ring.

'In my car, we'll be there in less than ten minutes.'

The car was a black and huge De Soto that I imagined was a '46 or '47 model. Inside, it smelled of enclosure and stale tobacco.

Mogaburu went around the corner and entered Dorrego. We soon reached Lacroze in Corrientes, Guzmán and we entered the inner roads of the Chacarita cemetery.

We stepped down and started walking along cobbled paths. My blessed or cursed literary curiosity urged me to follow him now through the area of the crypts without asking any questions. In one of them with the name MOGABURU on its facade, he introduced a key and opened the black iron door.

'Come on,' he said, 'don't be afraid.'

Although I didn't want to, I obeyed him, at the same time resenting his allusion to my supposed fear. I entered the crypt and descended a small metal ladder. I saw two coffins.

'In this box,' the man pointed to the lower lit, 'María Rosa, my wife, who died the same day Frondizi was made president.'

He tapped the top one several times with his knuckles.

'And this one belongs to my daughter, Mabel. She died, the poor thing, so young. She was barely fifteen when God took her away in May of 1945. Last month, it was fifteen years since her death. She would be 30 now.'

I felt my legs shaking, and a kind of very hard ball formed in my stomach.

'Unfair Death couldn't keep her away from her great passion, literature. She continued restlessly reading book after book. Can you see? Here is Mabel's other library, more complete and up to date than the one at home.'

True, one wall of the crypt was covered almost from the floor to the ceiling, I assume because of a lack of space, by hundreds of books, most of them in a horizontal position and in double rows.

'She, methodical person that she was, filled the shelves from top to bottom and left to right. Therefore, your book, being a recent borrowing, must be on the half full shelf on the right.'

A strange force led me to that shelf, and there it was, my *Don Segundo.*

'In general,' Mogaburu continued, 'not many people have come to claim the borrowed books. I can see you love them very much.'

I had fixed my eyes on the first page of *Don Segundo.* A very large green X blotted out my stamp and my annotation. Under it, with the same ink and the same careful writing in print letters, there were three lines:

Library of Mabel Mogaburu
Volume 5328
7th of June of 1960

'The bitch!' I thought. 'Think how earnestly I asked her not to write even a comma.'

'Well, that's the way things go,' the father was saying. 'Are you taking the book or leaving it as a donation to Mabel's library?'

'Of course I am taking it with me, I don't like getting rid of my books.'

'You are doing right,' he replied while we climbed the ladder. 'Anyway, Mabel will soon find another copy.'

THERE'S A MAN IN THE HABIT OF HITTING ME ON THE HEAD WITH AN UMBRELLA

There's a man in the habit of hitting me on the head with an umbrella. It makes exactly five years today that he's been hitting me on the head with his umbrella. At first, I couldn't stand it, now I'm used to it.

I don't know his name. I know he's average in appearance, wears a grey suit, is greying at the temples and has a common face. I met him five years ago, one sultry morning. I was sitting on a tree-shaded bench in Palermo Park, reading the paper. Suddenly, I felt something touch my head. It was the very same man who now, as I'm writing, keeps whacking me mechanically and impassively with an umbrella.

On that occasion, I turned around filled with indignation and he just kept on hitting me. I asked him if he was crazy, he didn't even seem to hear me. Then I threatened to call a policeman. Unperturbed, cool as a cucumber, he stuck with his task. After a few moments of indecision, and seeing that he was not about to change his attitude, I stood up and punched him in the nose. The man fell down and let out an almost inaudible moan. He immediately got back on his feet, apparently with great effort, and, without a word again, began hitting me on the head with the umbrella. His nose was bleeding, and, at that moment, I felt sorry for him. I felt remorse for having hit him so hard. After all, the man wasn't exactly bludgeoning me, he was merely tapping me lightly with his umbrella, not causing any pain at all. Of course, those taps were extremely bothersome. As we all know, when a fly lands on your forehead you don't feel any pain whatsoever, what you feel is annoyance. Well then, that umbrella was one humongous fly that kept landing on my head time after time and at regular intervals.

Convinced that I was dealing with a madman, I tried to escape. But the man followed me, wordlessly continuing to hit me. So I began to run (at this juncture I should point out that not many people run as fast as I do). He took off after me, vainly trying to land a blow. The man was huffing and puffing and gasping so, that I thought, if I continued to force him to run at that speed, my tormentor would drop dead right then and there.

That's why I slowed down to a walk. I looked at him. There was no trace of either gratitude or reproach on his face. He merely kept hitting me on the head with the umbrella. I thought of showing up at the police station and saying, 'Officer, this man is hitting me on the head with an umbrella.' It would have been an unprecedented case. The officer would have looked at me suspiciously, would have asked for my papers and begun asking embarrassing questions. And he might even have ended up placing me under arrest.

I thought it best to return home. I took the 67 bus. He, all the while hitting me with his umbrella, got on behind me. I took the first seat. He stood right beside me and held on to the railing with his left hand. With his right hand, he unrelentingly kept whacking me with that umbrella. At first, the passengers exchanged timid smiles. The driver began to observe us in the rear view mirror. Little by little, the bus trip turned into one great fit of laughter, an uproarious interminable fit of laughter. I was burning with shame. My persecutor, impervious to the laughter, continued to strike me.

I got off, we got off, at Pacífico Bridge. We walked along Santa Fe Avenue. Everyone stupidly turned to stare at us. It occurred to me to say to them, 'What are you looking at, you idiots? Haven't you ever seen a man hit another man on the head with an umbrella?' But it also occurred to me that they probably never had seen such a spectacle. Then five or six little boys began chasing after us, shouting like maniacs.

But I had a plan. Once I reached my house, I tried to slam the door in his face. That didn't happen. He must have read my mind because he firmly seized the doorknob and pushed his way in with me.

From that time on, he has continued to hit me on the head with his umbrella. As far as I can tell, he has never either slept or eaten anything. His sole activity consists of hitting me. He is with me in everything I do, even in my most intimate activities. I remember that at first the blows kept me awake all night. Now, I think it would be impossible for me to sleep without them.

Still and all, our relations have not always been good. I've asked him on many occasions and, in all possible tones, to explain his behaviour to me. To no avail, he has wordlessly continued to hit me on the head with his umbrella. Many times, I have let him have it with punches, kicks and even, God forgive me, umbrella blows. He would meekly accept the blows. He would accept them as though they were part of his job. And this is precisely the weirdest aspect of his personality, that unshakable faith in his work coupled with a complete lack of animosity. In short, that conviction that he was carrying out some secret mission that responded to a higher authority.

Despite his lack of physiological needs, I know that when I hit him, he feels pain. I know he is weak. I know he is mortal. I also know that I could be rid of him with a single bullet. What I don't know is if it would be better for that bullet to kill him or to kill me. Neither do I know if, when the two of us are dead, he might not continue to hit me on the head with his umbrella. In any event, this reasoning is pointless, I recognize that I would never dare to kill him or kill myself.

On the other hand, I have recently come to the realization that I couldn't live without those blows. Now, more and more frequently, a certain foreboding overcomes me. A new anxiety is eating at my soul. The anxiety which stems from the thought that this man, perhaps when I need him most, will depart and I will no longer feel those umbrella taps that helped me sleep so soundly

THE USHUAIA RABBIT

I just read this in a newspaper. 'After long months of futile attempts and several expeditions, a group of Argentine scientists has succeeded in capturing an Ushuaia rabbit, thought to be extinct for over a century. The scientists, headed by Dr. Adrián Bertoni, caught the rabbit in one of the many forests that surround the Patagonian city. . . .'

As I prefer specifics to generalities and precision to transience, I would have said 'in such and such a forest located in such a spot in relation to the capital of Tierra del Fuego.' But we can't expect blood from a turnip or any intelligence whatsoever from journalists. Dr. 'Adrián Bertoni' is yours truly, and, of course, they had to misspell my name. My exact name is Andrés Bertoldi, and I am, in fact, a doctor of natural sciences, specializing in Zoology and Extinct or Endangered, Species.

The Ushuaia rabbit is not actually a lagomorph, much less a leporid. It's not even certain that its habitat is the forests of Tierra del Fuego. Moreover, not one has ever lived on the Isla de los Estados. The rabbit I caught, I alone with no special equipment or help from anyone, showed up in the city of Buenos Aires near the embankment of the San Martín railroad, which runs parallel to Avenue Juan B. Justo where it crosses Soler Street in the district of Palermo.

Far from looking for the Ushuaia rabbit, I had other worries and was headed down the sidewalk of Juan B. Justo, a bit downcast. It was hot, and I had some unpleasant, not to say worrisome, business to do at the bank on Santa Fe Avenue. Between the embankment and the sidewalk, there is a wire mesh fence supported by a low wall, on the other side of the fence I spotted the Ushuaia rabbit.

I recognized it instantly, how could I not? But I was struck by the fact that it remained so still, for this animal is normally jumpy and restless. I thought it might be wounded.

Be that as it may, I backed up a few metres, climbed the fence and lowered myself catlike to the ground. I advanced stealthily, fearing at each moment that the Ushuaia rabbit would take fright and, in that case, who could catch it? It is one of the fastest animals in creation, though the cheetah is swifter in absolute terms, it is not in relative terms.

The Ushuaia rabbit turned and looked at me. Contrary to my expectations, however, it did not flee but kept still with the sole exception of the silver tuft of feathers that shook as if to challenge me.

I took off my shirt and waited, stock still and bare skinned.

'Easy, easy, easy...' I kept saying.

When I got close I slowly deployed the shirt as if it were a net and, suddenly, in one quick swoop, I had it over the rabbit, wrapping it up in a neat package. Using the sleeves and the shirt tail, I tied a strong knot, allowing me to hold the bundle in my right hand and use my left to negotiate the fence once more and return to the sidewalk.

I could not, of course, show up at the bank shirtless, much less with the Ushuaia rabbit. Thus, I headed home. I have an eighth floor apartment on Nicaragua Street between Carranza and Bonpland. At a hardware store, I picked up a birdcage of considerable size.

The doorkeeper was washing the sidewalk in front of our building. Seeing me bare chested with a cage in my left hand and a restless white bundle in my right, he looked at me with more astonishment than disapproval.

As bad luck would have it, a neighbour followed me in from the street and into the elevator. With her was her little dog, an ugly disgusting animal. Upon picking up the smell, unnoticed by human beings, of the Ushuaia rabbit, it erupted in earsplitting barks. On the eighth floor, I was able to rid myself of that woman and her stentorious nightmare.

I locked the door with my key, prepared the cage and, with infinite care, began unwrapping the shirt, trying not to upset, or worse, to hurt the Ushuaia rabbit. However, being shut in had angered it, and, when I opened the cage door, I couldn't stop the rabbit from hitting my arm with a stinger. I had sufficient presence of mind not to let the pain induce me to let go and I finally managed to manoeuvre it safely back into the cage.

In the bathroom, I washed the wound with soap and water and, right away, with medicinal alcohol. It then occurred to me that I ought to head to the pharmacy for a tetanus shot, which I did without wasting any time.

From the pharmacy, I went straight to the bank to conclude the cursed business that had been postponed because of the Ushuaia rabbit. On the way back, I picked up supplies.

Since it lacks a masticatory apparatus during the day, the most practical thing was to cut up the lights into little pieces and mix in some milk and chickpeas. I then stirred it all together with a wooden spoon. After sniffing the concoction, the Ushuaia rabbit absorbed it with no problem, just very slowly.

Its process of expansion begins at sunset. I, therefore, transferred the few pieces of living room furniture, two modest armchairs, a loveseat and an end table to the dining room, pushing them up against the dining table and chairs.

Before it was too big to get past the door, I made sure it left the cage. Now free and comfortable, it was able to grow as needed. In this new state, it completely lost its aggression and now became apathetic and lazy. When I saw its violet scales pop out, a sign of sleepiness, I headed for the bedroom, went to bed and called it a day.

The next morning, the Ushuaia rabbit had returned to the cage. In view of this docility, I felt it was unnecessary to shut the door. Let it decide when to be inside or out of its prison.

The instincts of the Ushuaia rabbit are infallible. Every evening it would leave the cage and expand like a fairly thick pudding on the living room floor.

As is well known, its faeces are produced at midnight on odd days. If one collects (in the spirit of play, naturally) these little green metallic polyhedrons in a sack and shakes them, they make a lovely sound with a rather Caribbean rhythm.

To tell the truth, I have little in common with Vanesa Gonçalves, my girlfriend. She is considerably different from me. Instead of admiring the many positive qualities of the Ushuaia rabbit, she thought best to skin it in order to have a fur coat made for herself. This can be done at night when the animal is elongated and the surface of its skin is broad enough that the cartilaginous ridges are displaced to the edges and don't get in the way of the incision and cutting. I did not want to help her do this operation. Armed with only dressmaking scissors, Vanesa relieved the Ushuaia rabbit of all the skin on its back. In the bathtub, with detergent and running water, a brush and bleach, she washed off any amber or bile that remained on the skin. Then she dried it with a towel, folded it, put it in a plastic bag and very happily took it off to her house.

It only takes eight to ten hours for the skin to completely regenerate. Vanesa had visions of a great scheme, each night she could skin the Ushuaia rabbit and sell its fur. I would not allow it. I did not want to convert a scientific discovery of such importance into a vulgar commercial enterprise.

However, an ecological society reported the deed, and a paid announcement came out in the papers accusing 'Valeria González' and, by association me, of cruelty to animals.

As I knew would happen, the onset of autumn restored the rabbit's telepathic language, and, although its cultural milieu is limited, we were able to have agreeable conversations and even to establish a kind of, how shall I say, code of coexistence.

The rabbit let me know that it was not partial to Vanesa, and I had no trouble understanding why. I asked my girlfriend not to come to the house any more.

Perhaps in gratitude, the Ushuaia rabbit perfected a way of expanding less at night so that I was able to bring all the furniture back to the living room. It sleeps on the loveseat and deposits its metallic polyhedrons on the rug. It never eats to excess and, in this as in everything else, its conduct is measured and worthy of praise and respect.

The rabbit's delicacy and efficiency reached the extreme of asking me what would be, for me, its ideal daytime size. I said I would have preferred the size of a cockroach but I realized that such a small size put the Ushuaia rabbit in danger of being stepped on (though not of being killed).

After several attempts, we decided that at night the Ushuaia rabbit would continue to expand to the size of a very large dog or even a leopard. During the day, the ideal would be that of a medium sized cat.

This allows me, when I am watching television, for example, to have the Ushuaia rabbit on my lap where I can stroke it absentmindedly. We have formed a solid friendship and sometimes we need only look at each other for mutual understanding. Nevertheless, these telepathic faculties that function during the winter months disappear with the first warm spells.

We are now in the last month of winter. The Ushuaia rabbit is aware that for the next six months it will not be able to ask me questions or make suggestions or receive advice or congratulations from me.

Lately, it's fallen into a kind of repetitive mania. It tells me, as if I didn't know, that it is the only surviving Ushuaia rabbit in the world. It knows it has no way of reproducing but, though I have asked many times, the rabbit has never said whether it is bothered by this or not.

Moreover, the rabbit continuously asks me every day and several times a day whether there is any use for it to go on living like this alone in the world, with me yes but without other creatures of its own kind. There is no way it can kill itself, and there is no way I could and, even if there were, I would never do it, kill such a sweet affectionate animal.

And so, as long as we experience the last cold spells of the year, I continue to converse with the Ushuaia rabbit, stroking it absentmindedly. When warm weather returns I shall only be able to stroke it.

THE VISITATION

In 1965, when I was twenty-three, I was training as a teacher of Spanish language and literature. Very early one morning at the beginning of spring, I was studying in my room in our fifth floor flat in the only apartment building on the block.

Feeling just a bit lazy, every now and again I let my eyes stray beyond the window. I could see the street and, on the opposite side, old Don Cesáreo's well kept garden. His house stood on the corner of a site that formed an irregular pentagon.

Next to Don Cesáreo's was a beautiful house belonging to the Bernasconis, a wonderful family who were always doing good and kindly things. They had three daughters, and I was in love with Adriana, the eldest. That was why from time to time I glanced at the opposite side of the street, more out of a sentimental habit than because I expected to see her at such an early hour.

As usual, Don Cesáreo was tending and watering his beloved garden, which was divided from the street by a low iron fence and three stone steps.

The street was so deserted that my attention was forcibly drawn to a man who appeared on the next block, heading our way on the same side as the houses of Don Cesáreo and the Bernasconis. How could I help but notice this man? He was a beggar or a tramp, a scarecrow draped in shreds and patches.

Bearded and thin, he wore a battered yellowish straw hat and, despite the heat, was wrapped in a bedraggled greyish overcoat. He was carrying a huge filthy bag, and I assumed it held the small coins and scraps of food he managed to beg.

I couldn't take my eyes off him. The tramp stopped in front

of Don Cesáreo's house and asked him something over the fence. Don Cesáreo was a bad tempered old codger. Without replying, he waved the beggar away. But the beggar, in a voice too low for me to hear, seemed insistent. Then, I distinctly heard Don Cesáreo shout out, 'Clear off and, once and for all, stop bothering me.'

The tramp, however, kept on and even went up the three steps and pushed open the iron gate a few inches. At this point, losing the last shred of his small supply of patience, Don Cesáreo gave the man a shove. Slipping, the beggar grabbed at the fence but missed it and fell to the ground. In that instant, his legs flew up in the air, and I heard the sharp crack of his skull striking the wet step.

Don Cesáreo ran on to the pavement, leaned over the beggar and felt his chest. Then, in a fright, he took the body by the feet and dragged it to the kerb. After that, he went into his house and closed the door, convinced that there had been no witnesses to his accidental crime.

Only I had seen it. Soon a man came along and stopped by the dead beggar. Then more and more people gathered, and at last the police came. Putting the tramp in an ambulance, they took him away.

That was it, the matter was never spoken of again.

For my part, I took care not to say a word. Maybe I was wrong but why should I tell on an old man who had never done me any harm. After all, he hadn't intended to kill the tramp, and it didn't seem right to me that a court case should embitter the last years of Don Cesáreo's life. The best thing, I thought, was to leave him alone with his conscience.

Little by little, I began to forget the episode but every time I saw Don Cesáreo it felt strange to realize that he was unaware that I was the only person in the world who knew his terrible secret. From then on, for some reason, I avoided him and never dared speak to him again.

* * *

In 1969, when I was twenty-six, I was working as a teacher of Spanish language and literature. Adriana Bernasconi had married not me but someone else who may not have loved and deserved her as much as I.

At the time, Adriana, who was pregnant, was very nearly due. She still lived in the same house and every day she grew more beautiful. Very early one oppressive summer morning, I found myself teaching a special class in grammar to some secondary school children who were preparing for their exams and, as usual, from time to time, I cast a rather melancholy glance across the road.

All at once, my heart literally did a flip-flop, and I thought I was seeing things.

From exactly the same direction as four years before, came the tramp Don Cesáreo had killed, the same ragged clothes, the greyish overcoat, the battered straw hat, the filthy bag.

Forgetting my pupils, I rushed to the window. The tramp had begun to slow his step, as if he had reached his destination.

He's come back to life, I thought, and he's going to take revenge on Don Cesáreo.

But the beggar passed the old man's gate and walked on. Stopping at Adriana Bernasconi's front door, he turned the knob and went inside.

'I'll be back in a moment,' I told my students and, half out of my mind with anxiety, I went down in the lift, dashed across the street and burst into Adriana's house.

'Hello!' her mother said, standing by the door as if about to go out. 'What a surprise to see you here!'

She had never looked on me in anything but a kindly way. She embraced and kissed me, and I did not quite understand what was going on. Then it dawned on me that Adriana had just become a mother and that they were all beside themselves with excitement. What else could I do but shake hands with my victorious rival?

I did not know how to put it to him and I wondered whether it might not be better to keep quiet. Then, I hit on a compromise. Casually, I said, 'As a matter of fact, I let myself in without ringing the bell because I thought I saw a tramp come in with a big dirty bag and I was afraid he meant to rob you.'

They all gaped at me. What tramp? what bag? robbery? They had been in the living room the whole time and had no idea what I was talking about.

'I must have made a mistake,' I said.

Then, they invited me into the room where Adriana and her baby were. I never know what to say on these occasions. I congratulated her, I kissed her, I admired the baby and I asked what they were going to name him. Gustavo, I was told, after his father. I would have preferred Fernando but I said nothing.

Back home, I thought, that was the tramp old Don Cesáreo killed, I'm sure of it. It's not revenge he's come back for but to be reborn as Adriana's son.

Two or three days later, however, this hypothesis struck me as ridiculous, and I put it out of my mind.

* * *

And would have forgotten it forever had something not come up in 1979 that brought it all back.

Having grown older and feeling less and less in control of things, I tried to focus my attention on a book I was reading beside the window, while letting my glance stray.

Gustavo, Adriana's son, was playing on the roof terrace of their house. Surely, at his age, the game he was playing was rather infantile, and I felt that the boy had inherited his father's scant intelligence and that, had he been my son, he would certainly have found a less foolish way of amusing himself.

He had placed a line of empty tin cans on the parapet and was trying to knock them off by throwing stones at them from a distance of ten or twelve feet. Of course, nearly all the pebbles were falling down into Don Cesáreo's garden next door. I could see that the old man, who wasn't there just then, would work himself into a fit the moment he found that some of his flowers had been damaged.

At that very instant, Don Cesáreo came out into the garden. He was, in point of fact, extremely old and he shuffled along putting one foot very carefully in front of the other. Slowly, timidly, he made his way to the garden gate and prepared to go down the three steps to the pavement.

At the same time, Gustavo, who couldn't see the old man, at last managed to hit one of the tin cans, which, bouncing off two or three ledges as it went, fell with a clatter into Don Cesáreo's garden. Startled, Don Cesáreo, who was halfway down the steps, made a sudden movement, slipped head over heels and cracked his skull against the lowest step.

I took all this in but the boy had not seen the old man nor had the old man seen the boy. For some reason, at that point Gustavo left the terrace. In a matter of seconds, a crowd of people surrounded Don Cesáreo's body, an accidental fall, obviously, had been the cause of his death.

The next day, I got up very early and immediately stationed myself at the window. In the pentagonal house, Don Cesáreo's wake was in full swing. On the pavement out in front, a small knot of people stood smoking and talking.

A moment later, in disgust and dismay, they drew aside when a beggar came out of Adriana Bernasconi's house, again dressed in rags, overcoat, straw hat and carrying a bag. He made his way through the circle of bystanders and slowly vanished into the distance the same way he had come from twice before.

At midday, sadly but with no surprise, I learned that

Gustavo's bed had been found empty that morning. The whole Bernasconi family launched a forlorn search, which, to this day, they continue in obstinate hope. I never had the courage to tell them to call it off.

TWO COMMON
MISCONCEPTIONS

One

Reasons for the Extinction of the Basilisks

The most casual observation would seem to suggest, beyond a doubt, that the basilisk species is on its way to extinction. Based on the studies conducted so far, it is clear that this is not the result of their persecution by the natives driven by their superstitions but is due rather to the length that these creatures require to carry out their reproductive cycles and the obstacles they encounter in that process.

It is patently untrue that the basilisks can kill with a mere glance. It is their custom instead to project from their eyes jets of blood. This blood produces on the skin of the person affected a type of ulcer or pustule that secretes an organic substance from which emerges a worm known scientifically as *Vermis basilisci* (Boitus). These worms thrive in the human body parasitically and gradually destroy the nervous system to the point that, in their final stage, they end up emptying the cranial cavity. This process can take from thirty five to forty years. The victim slowly loses control of his limbs and his senses and may even suffer premature death. The *vermis*, however, does not abandon the body until it has completely destroyed the encephalic mass. At this point, now acquiring the form of a kind of small snake, never measuring more than twenty centimetres in length, it leaves the cadaver and begins a slow migration toward the marshy regions. Few do, in fact, reach their destination since on their often lengthy trajectory they die of hunger or are devoured by crows or owls and also by small carnivorous mammals such as the sable, the ferret and the ermine. The small numbers of snakes that manage to survive complete their metamorphosis amidst the heat and humidity of the marshes from which, after a period that varies from five to six weeks, they then emerge transformed into basilisks. It is, to be sure, untrue that they are capable of killing with merely their glance.

Two

The Diet of Horses

Nor is it true that horses are exclusively herbivorous. Doctor Ludwig Boitus has proven that it was people of primitive societies who accustomed them to that condition. This was motivated by economic and, above all, safety concerns.

The fact is that in every horse exists a latent carnivorous instinct. Moreover, horses are the only animals that were originally carnivorous. The truth is that if they are fed a diet of only raw meat, the habits and appearance of the creatures undergo a transformation. Their innocent brown eyes acquire a malignant ochre cast, their front teeth lengthen and curve, their gait becomes sinuous and smooth, their movements tend to turn furtive, their talons, freed from the hooves, turn into claws. The horse is now the strongest, the largest, the fastest and most agile of all carnivorous animals.

Those primitive peoples who redirected to useful tasks the only ferocious animal that ravaged their villages came to realize, in time, that it was also desirable to blend into the world some sort of harmless horror. So, selecting several inoffensive, beautiful and useless animals that were accustomed to devouring their crops, they got them used to the taste of meat. Thus it was that what we know today as lions and tigers, panthers and jaguars came into being.

UNJUSTIFIED FEARS

I'm not very sociable and often I forget about my friends. After letting two years go by, on one of those January days in 1979, they're so hot, I went to visit a friend who suffers from somewhat unjustified fears. His name doesn't matter; let's just call him Enrique Viani.

On a certain Saturday in March 1977, his life changed course.

It seems that, while in the living room of his house near the door to the balcony Enrique Viani saw, suddenly, an 'enormous,' according to him, spider on his right shoe. No sooner had he had the thought that this was the biggest spider he'd seen in his life when, suddenly leaving its place on his shoe, the animal slipped up his pants leg between the leg and the pants.

Enrique Viani was, he said, 'petrified.' Nothing so disagreeable had ever happened to him. At that instant, he recalled two principles he had read somewhere or other, which were, 1) that without exception all spiders, even the smallest ones, carry poison and can inject it, and, 2) that spiders only sting when they feel attacked or disturbed. It was plain to see that huge spider must surely have plenty of poison in it, the full strength toxic type. So, Enrique Viani thought the most sensible thing to do was hold stock still since, at the least move of his, the insect would inject him with a definitive dose of deadly poison.

So, he kept rigid for five or six hours with the reasonable hope that the spider would eventually leave the spot it had taken up on his right tibia. Clearly, it couldn't stay too long in a place where it couldn't find any food.

As he came up with this optimistic prediction, he felt that indeed the visitor was starting to move. It was such a bulky heavy spider that Enrique Viani could feel and count the footfalls of the eight feet, hairy and slightly sticky, across the goose flesh of his leg. But, unfortunately, the guest was not leaving; instead, it nested with its warm and throbbing cephalothorax and abdomen in the hollow we all have behind our knees.

* * *

Up to here, we have the first and, of course, fundamental part of this story. After that, there came some not very significant variations. The basic fact was that Enrique Viani, afraid of getting stung, insisted on keeping stone still as long as need be, despite his wife and two daughters' pleas for him to abandon the plan. And so, they came to a stalemate where no progress was possible.

Then Graciela, the wife, did me the honour of calling me in to see if I could resolve the problem. This happened around two in the afternoon. I was a bit annoyed to have to give up my one siesta of the week and I silently cursed out people who can't manage their own affairs. Once over at Enrique Viani's house, I found a pathetic scene. He stood immobile, though not in too stiff a pose, rather like parade rest; Graciela and the girls were crying.

I managed to keep myself calm and tried to calm the three women as well. Then, I told Enrique Viani that if he agreed to my plan, I could make quick work of the invading spider. Opening his mouth just the least bit, so as not to send the slightest quiver through his leg muscle, Enrique Viani wondered, 'What plan?'

I explained. I'd take a razor blade and make a vertical slit downwards in his pants leg till I came to the spider, without even touching it. Once this was done, it would be easy for me to hit it with a rolled up newspaper, knock it to the floor and then kill it or catch it.

'No, no,' muttered Enrique Viani, desperate but trying to restrain himself. 'The pants leg will move, and the spider will sting me. No, no, that's a terrible idea.'

Stubborn people drive me up the wall. Without boasting, I can say my plan was perfect, and here this wretch who'd made me miss my siesta just up and rejects it for no serious reason and, to top it off, he's snotty about it.

'Then, I don't know what on earth we'll do,' said Graciela. 'And just tonight, we have Patricia's fifteenth birthday party...'

'Congratulations,' I said and kissed the birthday girl.

'... and we can't let the guests see Enrique standing there like a statue.'

'Besides, what will Alejandro say?'

'Who's Alejandro?'

'My boyfriend,' Patricia predictably answered.

'I've got an idea!' exclaimed Claudia, the little sister. 'We can call Don Nicola and...'

I want it clear that I wasn't exactly wild about Claudia's plan and had nothing to do with it being adopted. In fact, I was dead set against it. But everyone else was heartily in favour of it and Enrique Viani was more enthusiastic than anyone.

So Don Nicola showed up and right away, being a man of action and not words, he set to work. Quickly, he mixed mortar and brick by brick built up around Enrique Viani a tall thin cylinder. The tight fit of his living quarters, far from being a drawback, allowed Enrique Viani to sleep standing up with no fear of falling and losing his upright position. Then, Don Nicola carefully plastered over the construction, applied a base and painted it moss green to blend in with the carpeting and chairs.

Still, Graciela, dissatisfied with the general effect of this mini obelisk in the living room, tried putting a vase of flowers on top of it and then an ornamental lamp. Undecided, she said,

'This mess will have to do for now. Monday, I'll buy something decent looking.'

To keep Enrique Viani from getting too lonely, I thought of staying on for Patricia's party but the thought of facing the music our young people are so fond of terrified me. Anyway, Don Nicola had taken care to make a little rectangular window in front of Enrique Viani's eyes so he could keep entertained watching certain irregularities in the wall paint. So, seeing everything was normal, I said goodbye to the Vianis and Don Nicola and went back home.

* * *

In Buenos Aires, back in those years, we were all overwhelmed with duties and obligations. The truth is that I almost forgot all about Enrique Viani. Finally, a couple of weeks ago, I managed to get free for a moment and went to call on him.

I found he was still living in his little obelisk, only now a splendid blue flowering creeper had twined its runners and leaves all around it. I pulled a bit to one side some of the luxuriant greenery and through the little window I managed to spot a face so pale it was nearly transparent. Guessing the question I was about to ask, Graciela told me that through a kind of wise adaptation to the new circumstances nature had exempted Enrique Viani from all physical necessities.

I didn't want to leave without making one last plea for sanity. I asked Enrique Viani to be reasonable. After twenty-three months of being walled up, this spider of ours was surely dead, so, then, we could tear down Don Nicola's handiwork.

Enrique Viani had lost the power of speech or at any rate

his voice could no longer be heard, he just said no desperately with his eyes.

Tired and, maybe, a bit sad, I left.

In general, I don't think about Enrique Viani. But lately, I recalled his situation two or three times and I flared up with rebellion. Ah, if those unjustified fears didn't have such a hold, you'd see how I'd grab a pickaxe and knock down that ridiculous structure of Don Nicola's. You'd see how, facing facts that spoke louder than words, Enrique Viani would end up agreeing his fears were groundless.

But, after these flareups, respect for my fellow man wins out, and I realize I have no right to butt into other people's lives and deprive Enrique Viani of an advantage he so treasures.

WAITING FOR
A RESOLUTION

I am in the power of a mosquito. Were he so inclined, he would probably kill me. Luckily, until now, he has not abused his power. In the exercise of his sway over me, he is moderate, not the least bit capricious and, one might even say, constitutional. It must, however, be understood that my obedience derives not from a recognition of his qualities or virtues but from the fear he instils in me.

Were he to consider it expedient, he would kill me, and his crime, or execution, would go unpunished. In the event that the legal institutions could prove incontrovertibly that he was the murderer, they would not be able to punish him, not only because of the subsidiary fact that there is no provision in law for this type of offence but also because he would not allow it. To my great good fortune, I have common sense enough to see that he has once and for all dismissed the idea of doing away with me, so long as I give him no cause.

He has taken up residence on the wall near the top of an oil painting that depicts an improbable landscape in which two seemingly Spanish shepherdesses with great big crooks are deep in conversation about some topic or other (surrounded by a flock of mild looking sheep) one of whose straight back falls in with the line of the horizon in an unpleasing way. There is an abundance of topographical detail, a green plain, two purple mountains crowned with white and a blue river that empties into a greyish lake. I know next to nothing about fine art but this picture has always seemed to me to lack all aesthetic value. The mosquito, however, appears to have no interest in aesthetic values or, for that matter, in any other sort of value. At least, he has never shown either approval or disapproval.

He prefers to fill his time with other activities. In the morning, he enjoys an examination of the house, perhaps without set purpose. But the fact is that from the dining room, where he has established his seat of office, he goes first to the kitchen where apparently, but doubtless it's my imagination, he takes a special interest in the sparkle of a small saucepan with a long black handle. Sometimes, I wonder what attracts him about such an utterly vapid object but then I reason that when all is said and done he is only a mosquito. It's in the kitchen that he spends most of his time. Later, he wanders through the hall, the bedroom and the spare room, never lingering noticeably anywhere special. I think his aim is less to supervise the running of the house than to affirm his authority over his domains.

At midday, on the dot of half past twelve to be precise, he lunches. His diet varies little. Every day, he dines on a slice of Spanish blood pudding, which I serve him on a little china dish (he won't consider any other). I still remember the day he indignantly rejected a slice of Argentine blood pudding which, in my desire to please, I served him so as to curry favour. I had to rush out to the butcher's for his favourite and exclusive dish. As soon as I've left his meal on the table, I have to withdraw since he doesn't like anyone there when he's eating. I am not altogether without wit and, occasionally, when I have nothing more important to attend to, I spy on him through the keyhole. In point of fact, this is a rather foolish thing to do for I have to admit there is nothing especially remarkable in what I see. The moment the mosquito is certain that I have left the dining room, he descends in the unhurried manner that accords with his position and alights on the china dish. Then, he sticks his snout into the pudding and slowly and eagerly sips the blood (disdaining paradoxically the bits of nut that distinguish Spanish blood pudding from Argentine). No part of this activity differentiates him from any other mosquito in the world. Lunch usually takes two or three minutes. (Actually, I lied when I said that I watch him only when I have nothing more urgent to do. The truth is that I spy on him every day. It is a source of fascination to glimpse into the private lives of those in power.)

Once he has satisfied his hunger, he is overcome by lassitude and heaviness and apparently cannot return to his residence beside the sheep picture. At this point, he prefers a bit of a nap on the baseboard at exactly the spot where the paint has begun to flake. He wakes up at around five, making no further sorties through the house at this time. He sites himself beside the picture and stays there until dinner.

With regard to these details, I assumed wrongly that my precise knowledge of his daily habits would prove useful in ridding myself of him. I tried it only once, it turned out so badly I never dared try again. Events, it shames me even now to remember them, transpired in the following way.

On that occasion, it seemed to me that his lunch had lasted longer than usual and that the mosquito was particularly bloated. I slipped off my shoes and, arming myself with one of them, approached as noiselessly as possible, my heart in my mouth, until I stood over the baseboard where he slept or pretended to sleep. Blinded momentarily by arrogance, I honestly believed I could easily crush him against the wood of the baseboard with my shoe. But just as I was in the act of delivering the fatal blow, he took to the air with a speed not devoid of majesty and hurled himself in my face. Screaming with fear and half out of my mind, I set off in flight through the house. How quickly he flew, how skillfully he disguised himself against the dark background, how silent was his persecution, how many the obstacles that prevented my moving with the speed my perilous situation demanded. I tried to turn the key in the lock so as to open the door and flee my house forever but this simple operation was impossible. The mosquito gave me no time, the key wouldn't turn, my fingers seized up. I ran, I ran right through the whole house, I ran unable to put a closed door between him and me. I ran colliding with furniture, knocking over chairs, breaking vases and mirrors, tearing my clothes, barking my shins and stubbing my toes. I ran and ran and ran until, overcome by exhaustion and terror, I fell to my knees.

'Forgive me! Forgive me!' I cried, my clasped hands lifted in an attitude of prayer. 'I swear, I swear by everything holy I'll never try it again!'

The mosquito paused and began to revolve in smaller and smaller circles while I, weeping torrents, repeated the above and similar expressions. I don't know if he heard me. He seemed to be wondering what to do with me. He had to make an important decision for which, doubtless, he needed the reflection that only calm and quiet can provide. I, on the other hand, instead of remaining silent, kept whining, gasping and panting, my clothes drenched with sweat and, with all this, beginning to notice that the veins of my hands were swollen and blue, almost purple, almost black. The mosquito was thinking, meditating, deliberating. It was clear that he was in no haste to come to a decision he might later regret. He circled and circled, each time more slowly, as if he were going to stop, but the irritating thing was that he did not stop. This state of affairs lasted for more than half an hour while I (with dejected countenance, eyes full of tears, and trembling from head to foot, awaited his verdict and sentence, which would be delivered at the same time) looked through the window at the blurred shapes of the bricklayers at work on a construction site across the street, thinking that they were enjoying a world of sunshine, fresh air, buckets and simple bricks, a world where there was no place for a sinister all powerful mosquito who was about to deliberate on my life or death. In the end, the mosquito was merciful. With unutterable relief, I saw that he was slowly making his way back to the baseboard. He displayed not a trace of self-importance but he could be sure that never again would I dare harm him.

After this episode, I realized that I must resign myself to my fate. To be honest, he demands very little of me, only his two daily slices of blood pudding and the china dish. I have, nevertheless, one reservation. It upsets me, it wounds me and it humiliates me to be dominated by such a tiny creature, a creature that weighs less than a fraction of an ounce, when I weigh close to a hundred and eighty pounds. At the same time, I don't feel in the least humbled by having to bow to the control of an irrational being, one that has, literally, the brains of a mosquito. Perhaps my resignation is owed to the fact that I have often been bossed about by individuals who haven't the sense of a cat and a great deal less beauty.

But just as I have this one reservation, I also have one hope. I know that the life of a mosquito lasts but a few months. This is why each morning I cast a furtive glance at the calendar, waiting for the moment I can circle with my hidden red pencil the date the mosquito expires. On the other hand, tomorrow marks twenty years to the day since he began his reign. Apart from contradicting the laws of nature, the notion that the mosquito may be immortal engulfs me in a dimension of unreality.

If the mosquito is not immortal, there are two possible ways of accounting for the above facts. The first is that the mosquito has not always been the same one and that during the night, while I am asleep, the dying mosquito is replaced by a younger stronger mosquito. I was brought to this supposition one day by coming upon the body of a mosquito at the foot of my dining room table. To be sure, this is not conclusive evidence. I have no proof that this dead mosquito is the one that holds me in its power. It may have been just a common everyday mosquito like the ones so easily brought to heel with fly swatter and insecticide.

The second possibility excludes the first. The all powerful one might be the dead mosquito, and the mosquito beside the sheep picture a mere usurper with no power whatsoever whose authority is based on the simple fact of the office he holds and his resemblance to his predecessor. But since this argument does not explain my twenty years of domination, I must assume that the usurper mosquitoes are many and effect their substitution in an orderly fashion. Anyway, be that as it may, I cannot afford to be entirely convinced of this. It could prove fatal.

Meanwhile, as I can do nothing, days, months and years go by. Growing old, withering away in the grip of my own anxiety and to this very day dominated by a mosquito, I am still waiting for a resolution.

EPILOGUE
ABOUT MYSELF

I was born in the city of Buenos Aires on the 8th of November of 1942 to a lower middle-class family. My parents were second generation Argentineans but all my great-grand parents were Italian.

I am a Spanish Language and Literature teacher and I taught from 1968 until my retirement a few years ago. I was always inclined to read and later to try my hand at writing. In time, I had the luck to publish more than fifty-five books.

Literature has never been a source of anguish or metaphysical restlessness for me but the opposite, a source of inexhaustible pleasant moments. With such attitude of irresponsible hedonism, I read and reread the texts I like and, without the least remorse, I discard those that bore me or displease me regardless of the prestige or aura they might enjoy.

An identical principle guides my brain and my hand at the moment of inventing any kind of story. I write for the pleasure of writing and as long as the text does not put up too many hurdles. When I see that I cannot proceed with enough fluency I tell myself, 'This story wasn't destined for me,' and I discard it immediately.

I have often received messages from diverse readers that, with some variations, pose similar questions. For example:

'What did you want to symbolise with: a) the man that hits

another on his head with an umbrella? b) the mosquito that dominates the man, c) the fifty chastising lambs?'

In all cases my answers, in these or words like these, are;

When I write a story I try to make it the best possible story in a literary sense: I just want to write a story.

When I write a story I do not wish to symbolise anything at all or to picture an allegory of anything; neither do I try to build any kind of metaphor: I just want to write a story.

When I write a story I am not seeking to send any message of a moral or spiritual or social or political character or anything of anything: I just want to write a story.

When I write a story, my motivation is not to edify or shake the reader or make him vibrate in his ethics or turn him into a better man, a new worthier individual of our society, etcetera: I just want to write a story.

In a nutshell, when I write a story, I just want to write a story.

It follows that any symbols, metaphors, allegories, messages, invocations, moral inferences, sermons, advices, reprimands, teachings, etcetera, etcetera will be entirely at the risk of the readers own interpretation, and I do not accept the slightest responsibility for their decisions.

My first book was published in 1969 and it is called *La regresión zoológica,* and its stories are extremely poor. In contrast, I believe that those in the last book, *El crimen de san Alberto,* should not deserve death.

Fernando Sorrentino
Martínez (Buenos Aires), May 2013

CHRONOLOGY OF THE STORIES INCLUDED IN THIS VOLUME

The writing of these stories covers a period of approximately forty-five years. The chronological order refers to the date when they appeared for the first time in Spanish.

When two dates are shown, the first one refers to the date of the first publication of the text in some newspaper or magazine. The second one refers to its first inclusion in a book.

1978 and 1982	Piccirilli (Piccirilli)
1979 and 1982	Chastisement by the Lambs (La Corrección de los Corderos)
1979 and 1982	Unjustified Fears (Temores injustificados)
1983 and 2005	A Lifestyle (Un estilo de vida)
1983 and 2005	The Visitation (El regreso)
1994	Engineer Sismondi's Notebook (Cuaderno del ingeniero Sismondi)
1995 and 2005	Habits of the Artichoke (Costumbres del alcaucil)
1998 and 2005	Episode of Don Francisco Figueredo (Episodio de don Francisco Figueredo)
2005	A Life Perhaps Worth Restoring (Una existencia que quizá se restaure)
2006 and 2008	Problem Solved (Problema resuelto)
2007 and 2008	The Ushuaia Rabbit (El conejo de Ushuaia)
2008	The Cubelli Lagoon (La albufera de Cubelli)
2013	The Library of Mabel (La biblioteca de Mabel)

SOURCES OF THE FIRST PUBLICATION OF THE STORIES COLLECTED IN BOOKS

Of *Imperios y servidumbres*, Barcelona, Editorial Seix Barral, 1972: Cosas de vieja; En espera de una definición; Errores firmemente arraigados; Existe un hombre que tiene la costumbre de pegarme con un paraguas en la cabeza; Por culpa del doctor Moreau.

Of *El mejor de los mundos posibles,* Buenos Aires, Editorial Plus Ultra, 1976: Ambiciones ilegítimas; El Imperio de las Cotorritas; Mera sugestión; Un libro esclarecedor.

Of *En defensa propia*, Buenos Aires, Editorial de Belgrano, 1982: Esencia y atributo; Supersticiones retributivas; Para defenderse de los escorpiones; Piccirilli; La Corrección de los Corderos; Temores injustificados.

Of *El rigor de las desdichas,* Buenos Aires, Ediciones del Dock, 1994: Cuaderno del ingeniero Sismondi.

Of *El regreso. Y otros cuentos inquietantes*, Buenos Aires, Editorial Estrada, 2005: El regreso.

Of *Existe un hombre que tiene la costumbre de pegarme con un paraguas en la cabeza*, Barcelona, Ediciones Carena, 2005: Un estilo de vida; Costumbres del alcaucil; Episodio de don Francisco Figueredo; Una existencia que quizá se restaure.

Of *El crimen de san Alberto*, Buenos Aires, Editorial Losada, 2008: Problema resuelto; El conejo de Ushuaia.

SOURCES OF THE FIRST PUBLICATION OF THE STORIES NOT YET COLLECTED IN BOOKS

Of *Cuadernos del Minotauro*, year IV, n°. 6, Madrid, 2008: La albufera de Cubelli.

Of *Delicias al Día*, Valladolid, March 2013: La biblioteca de Mabel.